GATEWAYS THROUGH
STONE AND CIRCLE

GATEWAYS THROUGH STONE AND CIRCLE

A Manual of Evocation for the Planetary Intelligences

Frater Ashen Chassan F∴N∴F∴

Gateways Through Stone and Circle

ISBN: 978-0-9830639-3-3

2nd Printing

Published by Nephilim Press
A division of Nephilim Press LLC
www.nephilimpress.com

CONTENTS

DEDICATION

The completion of this work is dedicated to my wife, whose monumental patience has endured years of obsessive purchasing and creating of magical tools, weathering the effects of periodic communications with spirits gone awry, and hobbies which very few people understand in this day and age. In the day-to-day juggle of endless responsibilities, she has offered more assistance and support than I could ever repay. Her understanding of my paranormal pursuits and interests knows no bounds and she consistently supports me in my passion to fulfill the Great Work. It is by her efforts and suggestions that such interests of mine began to be written down. I am forever grateful for her coming into my life.

FOREWORD

This book was originally written for a group of magicians whose founding goal was to use their collective abilities to create an empowering and assisting *Thoughtform*. The intended purpose of this *egregore* was to generate health, prosperity, and abundance for everyone involved. The developing group wished to empower each member and, in effect, the world, so that all would be would be set to rights.

"Rights" in the sense that necessary health, abundance, wealth, and prosperity would be generated, developed and established in every aspect of manifested reality. Through the integration and adoration of the aspects of Jupiter, such ends are being realized.

The efforts of a few magicians soon blossomed into a working network of highly enthusiastic will-workers of various backgrounds and abilities. The "gentlemen" have become a cohesive group of independent practitioners who are all striving towards a common endeavor: the fullest realization of prosperity imaginable. It is from these magicians that this work was inspired, and it is to the honor of their order that I present this book to you.

In conjunction with celestial communication, the contacting and integrating of the classical, planetary intelligences and their attributes has been foremost in the group's workings, and none other so much as the Jupiterian (Jovian) angels, spirits, and godforms that act as patrons and are the archetype for the group's entire formation. While each magician has gone about his or her own way of contacting and experiencing these beings, most participants follow a similar model of practice. This common ritual is one which has been loosely adapted from a section listed in Francis Barrett's plagiarized masterpiece, *The Magus*. It is from this same work that the endeavor of this book is set upon.

An acknowledged co-founder of the group is a magician who led me to pursue this art to its fullest. I extend my sincerest gratitude to Frater Rufus Opus ("RO") and his inspired works, the research of which led to the inspiration to practice the art in earnest. For his generosity in giving *The Gentlemen for Jupiter* full access to his "Practical Planetary Magick" series and "Planetary Gateway" formulas, I am forever grateful.

I also wish to extend enormous gratitude to the respectable magicians who offered their time to review my original manuscript and offered feedback and reviews for its initial release. Their collective input made this work richer by far.

This book is my first attempt to present the sum of my research and experience of an art to a public audience, the purpose of which is aimed at exploring the traditional work of esoteric evocation and practicing it as closely to the written material as possible. The particular method of invocation/evocation concerned is:

The Magic and Philosophy of TRITHEMIUS OF SPANHEIM; containing his book of SECRET THINGS and DOCTRINE OF SPIRITS with many curious and rare secrets (hitherto not generally known;) THE ART OF DRAWING SPIRITS INTO CRYSTALS, &c.

With many other Experiments in the Occult Sciences, never yet published in the English Language and Translated from a valuable Latin manuscript, By Francis Barrett, Student of Chemistry, natural and occult philosophy, the Cabala, &c.[1]

Herein are my personal accounts, discoveries and workings with this system of magic, according to *The Magic and Philosophy of Trithemius of Spanheim*. In the pages below, I hope to take any interested magicians wishing to duplicate these experiments through each stage of development to ultimate success.

---

1 Francis Barrett, "The Magic and Philosophy of Trithemius of Spanheim," Joseph Peterson's Twilit

INTRODUCTION

The basic procedure for conducting the Trithemius experiment of *Drawing Spirits into Crystals* is fairly simple and straightforward. In the barest sense, the only equipment required is a round table with seven planetary names, their associated angels and symbols written in a double ring. A triangle is drawn or engraved in the center of the table and some scrying device (e.g., crystal ball, black mirror, bowl of dark water, etc.) is set in the very center. Typically, a time of preparation is undergone. Then, at the correct day and hour, the call/invocation is performed for the desired angel to appear while the magus (or scrying partner/medium) gazes at the scrying device.

If the above process seems complicated enough, then this book might be difficult to digest. Within the magical community, there are countless methods for contacting spiritual beings, each with their own techniques involved. Discussing every magician's preferred method for evocation is beyond the scope of this work and counters the purpose. I intended this writing to be geared towards the traditionalist or traditionalist-curious who desire to recreate a historic experiment of magical ritual. Although this is meant to be a "traditional" work of the aforementioned text, an experienced magician should also be able to find complementing value in other works. For example, there are wonderful rituals and beneficial ideas from what RO graciously gives in his *Gateway* series.

The original concept of this book was to instruct a serious practitioner of the occult arts in the ("by the book") method of *Drawing Spirits into Crystals* (DSIC) from one who has done just that. As it stands, I am still committed to that goal, but have elected to include additional methods, equipment, and information of aspects I use in my own practices. The reader may utilize or disregard these additions if they so choose.

My hope is that I will be able to guide you, step by step, in an understandable, in-depth and organized manner, which will lead you to the successful evocation/invocation of an angelic being. I chose the ritual designed by Trithemius due to its relatively straightforward and direct approach to angelic communication.

This work is *not* for someone who is simply anxious to experience magic and be dazzled by the results of minimal labor! Following any grimoire or classic magic text to the letter will take time, dedication, expenses, and patience to procure everything that is required. Magicians who have already worked with various forms of ritual magic (modified or not) and are seriously interested in trying this "by the book" approach will find much enjoyment ahead. It's an investment of no small degree and demands the time and the attention to reap the rewards. My experience in this sort of endeavor has been that the amount of work done is proportional to the degree of benefits or experiences received.

Disclaimer

Let me state that I have neither the desire nor intention to present my work as the only legitimate method of practicing *The Art of Drawing Spirits into Crystals* while condemning anything contrary as false or "New Age." I express with certainty the things that work in my operations while leaving unexplored elements open for the reader to explore. I am quite familiar with what makes sense and seems probable in this art, and also with what seems silly and far-fetched.

I do not consider myself an ambassador of legitimate grimoric magic; I simply endeavor to work as closely to the text as ethically and as earnestly as possible. I try to discover what the wisdom of my predecessors can offer before jumping to egotistical conclusions and altering procedures prematurely. Testament to my passion and appreciation for grimoric magic and the resulting experience can hopefully be seen in the following sections. I have invested heavily in materials, time, and trial to reproduce the experiments as closely as I was able. In this practice, I find my experimentation continues to evolve and progress as my experience increases.

CHAPTER I

WORKING FROM THE GRIMOIRES: A METHOD TO THE MADNESS

I n attempting to reproduce the procedures and results which are written about in any given book of magic, I often reread the text many times until I am able to visualize the entire experiment, from beginning to end. I continue to do this until I am able to feel myself performing each action without missing a single step. Frequently, I reconsider sections of a ritual I was previously sure about only to realize the author was intending something else entirely. A magician's assumptions about any part of a ritual can make the difference between a successful evocation and an unsuccessful evocation.

I do not make any guarantees for success; I only can recount what I've experienced for myself. Any deviations or substitutes from what is written in the original text will be on the will (head) of the magician. This applies to the changes I myself have made. I advise against adding or substituting any implements or methods described in other grimoires or used in other magical practices unless they are directly applicable.

In many instances, I've heard modern magicians complain about what is "comfortable" or more "compatible" for them in regards to conducting grimoric experiments. In considering any art or practice, it is better that you "empty your cup" and assume nothing. This is vital so as not to miss any crucial element of working which the art contains. In the practice of evoking spirits, there is no room for frivolity or cutting corners if one expects to really succeed. Each part of the ritual, each piece of equipment, every invocation, is part of a whole and has a specific purpose. Whether or not you're comfortable with any of these or believe they are needed is irrelevant.

Researching the minds which birthed the classical texts of magic will help bring its methods to fuller understanding. Unless you are quite familiar with the thinking and culture of Renaissance Europe, many elements of grimoric ritual might seem foreign or bizarre. To understand the procedure for *Drawing Spirits into Crystals*, understanding the author of the original text is a helpful way to begin.

HISTORY

Francis Barrett credits an abbot named Johannes Trithemius (treh-TA-mee-us) of Spanheim for being the author of *Drawing Spirits into Crystals*. Without question, Trithemius is one of the most prominent figures in western occultism. He is responsible for numerous esoteric works, as well as notorious for his ingeniously encrypted messages hidden within his volumes of writing.

We can only speculate if Trithemius is indeed the one responsible for the particular experiment of DSIC as it is given in *The Magus*. It may be that Barrett created the experiment himself, utilizing techniques taught by Trithemius and further recorded by Cornelius Agrippa. Barrett may have decided to capitalize on Trithemius' name much the same way as other magicians ascribed Solomon or Moses to their own works. It is even more likely that Barrett compiled the DSIC operation from older texts, which may or may not have been influenced by Trithemius. He was known to have had access to quite a few magical works in his library.

Of noteworthy attention are two magical texts which are not widely known. The manuscripts in question were both transcribed by a man named Frederick Hockley (1808–1885). Hockley worked for a bookseller named John Denley who was acquainted with Francis Barrett. It was from this bookseller that Barrett collected many magical works he would compile into his masterpiece, *The Magus*.

The two manuscripts Hockley transcribed show elements used in the DSIC experiment, and one is most certainly taken from the same source as our DSIC. It is quite obvious to me that the manuscripts each originated from a common ancestor and had been modified further by whoever transcribed the original. In *A Complete Book of Magic Science,* of which Hockley made numerous copies, we find sections borrowed from at least four different magical texts. The same invocations used in DSIC can be found within this manuscript, sometimes written word for word, and largely, the same set of interrogative questions located near the end. Pictures of the tools are also included which obviously resemble the ones in *The Magus.* The entire procedure of DSIC is directly in line with how *A Complete Book of Magic Science* reads. It encompasses what is known as the *Grimoire of Turiel,* a small grimoire of angelic evocation of uncertain origin. I highly recommend a study of this short grimoire to further understand how DSIC is to be performed.

The second work is titled *Occult Spells: A Nineteenth Century Grimoire,* and has a section describing a "Consecrated Beryll stone... set in a ring or circle of silver." This instrument is similar to the enclosure used in DSIC, which was an ebony pedestal containing the crystal stone encompassed by the gold plate. The diagram of the angelic names within the disk is practically identical between *Occult Spells* and Trithemius. The crystal stone, ebony pedestal, and other equipment will be treated in depth in Chapter IV.

Regardless of the exact origin, it is Trithemius of Spanheim who is credited as the author of *The Art of Drawing Spirits into Crystals.* The historical ambiguity of the operation does nothing to discredit its validity. The text appears to be harmonious with the other writings of Trithemius and is presented in a similar context of his thought and practice; planetary angels were quite familiar to the mystical abbot. His life, no doubt, earned him the level of fame he achieved within the occult community as a founding father of western occultism.

"Trithemius was first and foremost a Christian monk, a member of the Benedictine order; who dedicated his life to fulfilling the requirements of monastic piety. Secondly, Trithemius was an exceptionally erudite monk, who as the abbot of two monasteries during his lifetime, zealously advocated in the pursuance of his monastic goals, not piety alone, but *learned* piety."

Christened Johann Heidenberg, Trithemius acquired his Latin name from his birthplace of Trittenheim on the banks of the Mosel. Trithemius left home at the age of fifteen after having a dream that he was destined to "live a life of letters" and went to pursue an education in Heidelberg.

After completing his studies there in 1482, Trithemius decided to travel back to the Mosel valley but ended up getting caught up in a snow storm on the way. He took shelter in a nearby Benedictine monastery in Sponheim where he decided to remain after believing he was lead there by divine providence. He continued to stay and learn there until he became the monastery's abbot at the age of twenty-one. He would continue to serve there as abbot for the next twenty-three years.

In a letter that was originally intended to reach a monk by the name of Arnold Bostius, Carmelite monk of Ghent, Trithemius wrote that he indeed was an "exponent of the occult arts." The occult subject matter he claimed to be a worker of was the art of steganography, or "the art of writing secret messages and transmitting them over long distances through the mediation of angelic messengers." Unfortunately, his intended recipient had died before reading the letter and it fell into another who made public knowledge of Trithemius' dealings with spirits. He is believed to have possessed some of the greatest grimoires of the time, including the five books of *Lemegeton,* and most notably, *Liber Malorum Spirituum,* or "Book of Names and Seals of Evil Spirits," which would eventually become known as the *Goetia.* Much of what is found in four of the five books of *Lemegeton* can be attributed to Trithemius. His work would eventually have considerable influence on some of the most renowned magicians of the renascence era, namely Heinrich Cornelius Agrippa (1486–1535) and Paracelsus (1493–1541).

Much of Trithemius' published work focuses on methods for utilizing angels and crystallomancy to send messages between magicians. Enciphered within these writings are discussions of cryptography and steganography, and these are often thought to be the real purpose of the texts. I would suggest that the cryptographic techniques may have been taught or inspired by the angels rather than supplanting them. Nevertheless, Trithemius' involvement in and contribution to not only the occult but other sciences of the time was remarkable.

Regardless of his scholarly pursuits, his studies eventually brought him more grief than praise. Suspicions of his knowledge and his reputation as a magician grew, eventually isolating him from the other monks. Trithemius eventually resigned as abbot in 1506. Sometime following his departure, he took up an offer from the Bishop of Würzburg, Lorenz von Bibra, to become the abbot of St. James's Abbey in Würzburg. He continued on there until his death.

Steganographia would become one of Trithemius' most infamous and influential writings. It is an extensive work of three volumes which contains meticulous instructions for the evocation of spirits, particularly angels in order transmute messages over long distances. These volumes were eventually found to contain the codes to decipher his extensive cryptic messages, which are hidden through his numerous writings.

Thethimius' other works include *De Laude Scriptorum* (In Praise of Scribes) (written 1492, printed 1494), *Annales Hirsaugiensis* (1514), *Polygraphiae* (1518), and *De Septum Secundeis* (The Seven Secondary Intelligences, 1508), a history of the world based on astrology. This last work has particular correlation and relation to our experiment of DSIC. In this manuscript, Trithemius relates the history of the world to the Emperor of Rome.

In *De Septum Secundeis*, or *The Seven Secondary Intelligences*, Trithemius describes seven planetary angels who ruled for 354 years and four months each. According to Trithemius, the workings of humanity, whether progressive or profane, were overseen by a particular ruling angel at these given times in history. An interesting contrast to DSIC is that the order in which each angel governs is different. Also, the names used for some of the angels differ between the two works, although this is fairly common in occult literature.

In *De Septum Secundeis*, the world of creation begins with the Saturnian Archangel, Orifiel, ruling for the first 354 years. During this time, Trithemius describes mankind as existing in the most primitive of manners, being close to nature while learning the workings of creation around them. The Archangel of Venus, Anael, takes over after Orifiel and mankind make leaps and bounds with music, the making of clothes, and of course, indulgences in carnal desires.

Three hundred fifty-four years and four months later, Zachariel of Jupiter assumed command and Trithemius describes the great accomplishments made by mankind in ruling, hunting, luxury, divisions of nations, politics, and law. Raphael, as the Archangel of Mercury, rules writing, music, communication, and travel to distant lands; all are recited as man's achievements under this Archangel's rule. Next, Samuel (Samael) of Mars was said to encourage men to establish dominant monarchies, religions, and kingdoms and also to wage war.

The next age brought the rule of Gabriel of the Moon, bringing the building of cities and increased populations across the earth. Finally came Michael's time to rule, bringing greater accomplishments in the areas of mathematics, astronomy, and other sciences. After 354 years and four more months of rule, the cycle begins anew with Orifiel once again taking command.

The account of *The Secondary Intelligences* is intriguing, but also suspiciously vague concerning details. Most likely, Trithemius was once again concealing hidden messages within the repeated numbers and sequences. If we accept this system of rulers, the current Archangel for our present time is Michael. His governorship will last until the year 2233. *De Septum Secundeis* holds relevance to the magician of the DSIC operation as it alludes to aspects of the human condition which may be enhanced under particular angels.

Trithemius is responsible for many other works, most of which have concealed within them his ciphered messages and playful antics. More noteworthy accomplishments are:

Annales Hirsaugiensis. The full title is Annales hirsaugiensis... complectens historiam Franciae et Germaniae, gesta imperatorum, regum, principum, episcoporum, abbatum, et illustrium virorum, Latin for "The Annals of Hirsau ... including the history of France and Germany, the exploits of the emperors, kings, princes, bishops, abbots, and illustrious men." Hirsau was a monastery near Württemberg, whose abbot commissioned the work in 1495, but it took Trithemius until 1514 to finish the two volumes, 1400 page work. It was first printed in 1690. Some consider this work to be one of the first humanist history books.

The Cipher Manuscripts are a collection of 60 folios that were encrypted by using the Trithemius cipher. The data that was encrypted were working notes made by someone with knowledge of ceremonies from a German Rosicrucian temple.[4] In September 1887, they were deciphered by William Wynn Westcott and later used as the basis for rituals of initiation into the **Golden Dawn.**

What must be thoroughly understood and accepted by any magician wishing to emulate experiments of classical era magic are the unrelenting Christian overtones. Religious saturation is prevalent in every aspect of not only the procedure, but the belief and social position of the magicians who practiced them. Noel Brann, in his excellent study of Trithemius, observes:

What is true of all of the Renaissance Magi, with the possible exception of Giordano Bruno, is their adherence to Christianity, albeit of a rather heterodox nature. This insistence on the consonance between magic and Christianity is particularly pronounced in Trithemius, a Benedictine Abbot.[2]

Keep in mind the nature of the rituals and the beliefs of the magician who designed them. Trithemius was a devout Christian. To him, as well as many magicians of the era, magic was a sacred and holy art under the God and the religion they followed. Trithemius declares this clearly, writing regarding magic:

> *The word magic is the Persian term for what in Latin is called wisdom, on which account magicians are called wise men, just as were those three wise men who, according to the Gospel, journeyed from the East to adore, in his crib, the infant who was the Son of God in the flesh.*[3]

The entire assortment of magical equipment and conjurations are designed within a Judeo-Christian cosmology. Treating them as anything contrary would be a contradiction of intentions that could negatively impact your experiments. Although I do not condone reinventing your belief system to the similitude of preindustrial era monks, hostility toward such beliefs, past or present, will not assist you in grimoric arts. For the aspiring grimoric magician, the section of the *Fourth Book of Occult Philosophy* titled "The Invocation of Good and Evil Spirits" should be thoroughly read and comprehended before continuing any further:

> *The good spirits may be invoked of us, divers ways, and in sundry manners do offer themselves unto us. For they do openly speak to those that watch [a person who is a seer or scryer], and do offer themselves to our sight, or do inform us in dreams by oracle of those things which are desired. Whosoever therefore would call any good spirit, to speak or appear in sight, it behoveth them especially to observe two things: one whereof is about the disposition of the invocant; the other about those things which are outwardly to be adhibited to the invocation, for the conformity of the spirits to be called. It behoveth therefore that the invocant himself be religiously disposed for many days to*

---

2   Brann, Noel L., *Trithemius and Magical Theology* (Albany: SUNY, 1999), p. 115.
3   Ibid., p. 11.

such a mystery. In the first place therefore, he ought to be confessed and contrite, both inwardly and outwardly, and rightly expiated, by daily washing himself with holy water. Moreover, the invocant ought to conserve himself all these days, chaste, abstinent, and to separate himself as much as may be done, from all perturbation of mind, and from all manner of forraign and secular business…[4]

There is something to be said for the dedication, discipline, and time involved in the working of any historic system. It allows you to integrate previously foreign material and make it your own. Removing a magical formula from its religious, cultural, and spiritual context is a sure way to strip the entire experiment of its integrity and intended purpose. Regardless of your spiritual preferences, respect should be shown to any historic art form. Nevertheless, I have come to the conclusion that it is eventually appropriate to alter a magical operation once you have worked the given formulae to the letter and put its practice to repeated experimentation first.

Preparation for grimoric work was and is a serious undertaking. Only after real experience working from a traditional source can you claim what does and does not work for you. This is what separates the grimoric armchair theorist from the true working magician. So, if you are a mage who is dedicated to seeing this experiment through, I congratulate you and lend my wishes for your greatest success! Now, let's get down to business.

---

4   Skinner, Stephen (ed.), *Fourth Book of Occult Philosophy,* (Berwick, ME: Ibis, 2005)..

CHAPTER II

THE MAGICIAN'S USE OF MAGIC

xactly how magicians harness their *will* and focus their attention says a lot about how they perceive themselves and the surrounding world. *Magic* has undergone many definitions and explanations by the interested minds of our time; similar to dreams or faith, magic is inherently unique to each human being who experiences it. The integration and utilization of concepts which go beyond purely rational and conscious reasoning are the mechanisms a magician directs with intrinsic will. Whether spurred by faith, idealism, or raw passion, the vehicle to express magic requires something specific to the soul of the magician.

The manipulation of numerous strands of symbolic patterns, frequencies, and sublime powers requires a gifted and disciplined mind. All of this must be brought to a single focus to manifest the desired outcome into an actualized result. Dedication and perseverance to see any magical act through to completion takes an act of supreme will.

Nothing in magic ritual should be done mundanely or lacking in reverence for the symbolism of the ritual. Although understanding grows with successful experience, never assume to be above the dictates of a ritual. There will be little success in following magical procedure without true appreciation for each of its components.

It is fine to speculate and theorize about the true nature of a magical experience before or after one has experienced it, but not during. There is no benefit in undertaking magical rituals with a dozen different conflicting ideals and philosophies about *who* makes *what* work and *why*. Nothing is concrete, even in the sciences. There are continually changing variables within the scope of human comprehension. For me, experiencing an angel is much more important and personally beneficial than properly defining what an angel is. It is also much more fulfilling than trying to prove a magical or philosophical *ideal.*

In the act of magical evocation — and most certainly, invocation — the magician is not an objective observer, separate from the experience he is involved in. I've found that trying to rationally dissect the occurrences of a magical ritual as they occur is a sure way to *short out* the entire experience. During my evocations, the times when I felt I was most successful were when my expectations and assumptions were set aside. The only desire I had was to achieve the purpose of the ritual: the appearance and interaction with the spirit I was calling forth. Even after completion of a ritual, I found that some of the things I was told weren't to be understood until later. Profound wishes and desires can be manifested through your requests to these beings, but I've found the true treasure lies in the intrinsic alterations which take place within the magician.

Most practitioners or researchers in the arts of evocation are familiar with the debate as to whether conjured spirits are either internal or external manifestations. I've read the debates for both and theorize that the answer lies somewhere in between. I hold that the spirits and beings we have encounters with in the world and summon to our circles definitely exist, but our experience of them is colored and sometimes limited by the interpretations of our physical minds. I find it rather silly when people describe things which are not physical in a purely corporeal representation. There is no reason for a spirit or any other nonphysical being to "look" like anything at all. Physical appearances, even in the world of matter, are but a tiny sliver of truth. In the spiritual, when we "see" something, it is not simply light reflecting off of matter into our eyes; the experience relies on a different sense (or possibly a combination of senses) which our minds then attempt to comprehend.

THE GOAL OF THE WORK

Despite what anyone assumes or has said about this art, it should be understood that the purpose of this work is the complete evocation/invocation of planetary beings (in this case an angel) to visible and audible presence. This is accomplished through the methods of the ritual and through a successful connection to the desired entity. Communication will occur directly or through a scryer, catalyzed by the ceremony. The possible results of the ritual are numerous, but may include the attainment of knowledge, integration of archetypal virtues, or discovery of the occult. Each of the planetary intelligences has something unique to offer and new ways in which to harness the aptitudes of the celestial spheres within yourself. This is not to assume that every angel will be beneficial to you or respond the way you might want. Often angels challenge us to uproot our destructive patterns and move beyond self-imposed limitations.

I tend to use the terms "invocation" and "evocation" interchangeably in this art, due to the nature of the beings which are being summoned. To elaborate further requires an understanding of how angels present themselves to us. To say a magician can call down an agent of the working universe to do their bidding while taking them away from their designated function is a bit naïve. I can say with no lack of certainty that I have never "evoked" the full manifestation of the Archangel Michael to my circle within the crystal sphere. Despite this, I am equally certain that the same angel arrived and was fully present during my conjuration. The paradoxical truth of this has to do with the nature of beings that are highly ascended in the spiritual order. I'll explain more about my personal interactions with angelic entities presently.

First of all, know that time and space has no bearing on angelic beings as they do for physical beings. The answer to the infamous question, "How many angels can dance on the head of a pin" is this: As many as would care to. Their presence has no measurable physical equivalent besides the reaction of others to their presence. Although I cannot fully comprehend nor explain how it works, such mighty beings are able to directly communicate with us without flooding us with the magnitude of their full presence. Archangel Michael — whose name translates closest to "He who is unto the likeness of God" — is seen as one of the most powerful angels assisting the works of Creation.

When I explain evocation below, I refer specifically to the calling of an entity beyond your personal sphere yet within your midst. How much of the angel you or your scryer is able to perceive seems to correlate directly with how much a person can handle.

In the DSIC operation, Archangel Michael is attributed to the Sun. Six other mighty Archangels of biblical text or lore are ascribed to the other planets. These seven planetary angels are the main celestial beings you will be working with. Trithemius only briefly mentions it in the text, but writes that this art is also appropriate for the conjuration of the lesser planetary intelligences and demons, as well as other spirits.

In the next section, I will relate my personal experiences with the angels, as well as their classical correspondences. The popular (mis) conceptions of angels are as white-robed, typically blonde and beautiful humanoids with large wings that shine with joyful tenderness. They sound trumpets, sport halos, grant wishes, and banish evil. Within the myriad of western cultures and beliefs all sorts of folklore are associated with these mighty beings. Yet, even the Bible does not share modern day stereotypes of these holy messengers. I promise you that no media portrayal will match your own personal observation and interaction with them.

THE EQUATION OF TRADITIONAL WESTERN CEREMONIAL MAGIC

The reasons why the grimoric rituals worked for the magicians of old, as well as why they do for us today, is contained within the parameters set by the ceremony and the magician him/herself:

Scholarly research has shown that no historic book of magic is self-encompassed work. The rituals and procedures of historic books of magic have undergone a wide variety of inclusions as well as exclusions, translations, and interpretations. Grimoires are far from being unique in this as historic works in just about every written manuscript has undergone these types of changes. Each and every one has been altered by scribes and through the many hands which have translated them.

Many of the prayers and procedures located in medieval books of magic have undergone variation and many of the Spirit's names have been badly translated, misconstrued, and recopied over the years. It is prudent to assume that many of the scribes of the grimoires may have never actually performed the ceremonies (or at least not contacted each and every one of the spirits!) and therefore, may have never had any real interaction or new information to record their corrections in the material they were recopying. They were simply recopying works they had in their possession. Many of these same scribes recopied names and particular details inaccurately either as a result of human error or a deliberate alteration.

The question arises, then, "If this is true, then how were and are magicians able to successfully conjure spirits to visible appearance with these obvious alterations and/or mistakes in them?"

When acquaintances from foreign countries call my name, it is barely discernible and hardly relatable to my native English way of saying it, but I always know they are talking to me. Another profound example of this is the name *Jesus*. A name so well known, so widely used, so profound, and not even close to original sound or spelling from the language where the name originated from. However, it is widely believed and assumed that *Jesus* knows he is being contacted despite the mistranslation.

The answer to the above question may be further understood in the seemingly complex arrangement of dependent variables. I hope to explain this "equation of principles" in the most comprehensive and clear way possible.

If the correct numbers of elements are in alignment and the magician has the focused and supported will, the intended and desired results of the ritual can be accomplished. Keep in mind that historic dealings with spirits, as well as modern ones, are concerned with asking the spirit of the proper pronunciation and spelling of its name even when that name is believed to be known. So, the question arises, "How does the correct spirit arrive or even care to arrive when the magician calls the spirit by an incorrectly pronounced name?"

I believe the answer is an involved, yet simple combination of four crucial concepts, or principles, which must be integrated and harmonized to produce the desired results.

The first is *Divine Assistance* — The resulting strength of this conduit begins (and is determined) by Divine assistance (God/HGA, ascended intellect assists past some variables of human error) extending through the direct will of the magician to contact a particular spirit (or succeed in another magical or mystical endeavor). This is the nexus-relationship the magician desires through the purification, devoutness, and a divine connection within a state of unquestionable covenant that cannot be truly defined nor debated by those who have not experienced it. This state has no dogmatic or cultural boundaries; rather, it is a very specific state of being that must be in agreement with the magician's true being. It is a grace granted to the magician beyond any set formula or circumstantial prediction.

The second fundamental principle is the *Magician's Will* — This is probably one of the most difficult phenomena to explain. Crowley and a few others have done a good job of defining how the will, or "magic(k)," work, but there is one that I'm sure most people are familiar with. To paraphrase, the true will of the magician is the harmonious expression of complete being in all bodies. This is perhaps best explained by the multitude of sacred Trinities, the 3 of creation made 1: Father–Son–Holy Spirit, Thought–Word–Deed, Mind–Body–Soul, Heaven–Earth–Hell, Mental–Physical–Emotional, etc. When we are able to cancel the division between these "three" by pointed action, we get "magic" that is the whole of our comprehended universe.

The third principles are grouped together as:

> *The Spirit's Name; its Sigil, or Seal; it's Description, or Representation; and Time of Office.*

You'll hear modern Catholic exorcists and religious officials declare, "Once you know the demon's name, you will have power over it." Oddly, most of these same clergymen don't know *why* they would or could have power over it. Luckily, we, as magicians (well, at least some of us), know why this is so. As our arts reveal, if we know the "name" of a thing or spirit, we will hopefully be able to apprehend some of the meaning, and also (more importantly), how to devise a physical representation {"symbol/sigil"} to act as a direct embodiment — corresponding link. Also, if there is physical description of how the spirit should appear, we have further identifying traits to utilize. Thus, by representing a spiritual being's concept with a physical or visual counterpart, we are bridging the gap of the world of spirit and the world of form.

The magician utilizes the spirit's sigil even beyond its name to initiate this contact. This is why the *Goetia* of *Lemegeton* has most likely garnered much of its popularity. The spirit's sigil is its binding representation that singles it out from obscurity and isolates it to point of contact. For example, with the name "Jesus," we know we are talking about YESHUA when the symbol of the cross is involved and not a Mexican citizen. When multiplied with a relative description and appropriate time when the spirit is to be called, we, thus, narrow down the possibilities severely if there is indeed a spirit approximate to the grimoire's description.

The fourth and final principle to be integrated is the *Ritual Contract*: Namely the Conjurations — This is a deciding factor that the ritual will have validity in the dictates of its conjurations and ceremonies. This is where the magician personally does away with allowances for relativity, guile, vagueness, loose interpretation, and so on. If the magician feels they are acting in accordance with divine assistance, the words they speak in the context of the ceremony/ritual will have very severe authority and consequence.

We have been referring to the grimoires in a broad sense since each seems to come with specific conjurations or dictates as to what the summoned spirit is supposed to do. Typically, we take for granted that the magician is a holy man, designated spiritual authority and ordained as an exorcist as the book claims and thusly will "bind the spirit by oath and contract." This is where the magician/exorcist states (in no sense of vague interpretation) that the spirit will: appear visibly, speak according to the magician's understanding, be present and fulfill the wishes and commands of the exorcist, and act according to his benefit. In the cases of our grimoire, the above still applies; however, the magician is speaking with a divine being (an Archangel), so the tone is direct, but highly respectful. This is important to adhere to when working the DSIC operation.

If the above is accomplished successfully, a modern magician should confirm the correct name and pronunciation of the Spirit. This was possibly a less important aspect for the period magician if they felt they achieved successful evocation with how they were saying the spirit's name to begin with. However, if veritable contact with a spiritual entity is achieved, then such questions should not be omitted by the thorough magician.

Coming face to face with a spiritual being for the first time can be quite a shock to the mind of the modern magician. This is no doubt amplified in current times relative to the belief system of the magicians of old. Once you personally observe a spirit taking on a shape and appearance like that which the grimoires describe, you begin to accept that at least one of the magicians of the grimoires actually recorded what they observed. Also, many grimoires have a variety of examples about how spirits might appear and are thusly not so concrete as to not allow for variation. It does, however, give description and detail enough to know whether or not the correct entity has been contacted. It is the author's speculation that many of the names which were recorded in the grimoires were done so phonetically within the parameters of those magicians' linguistic and cultural capacities/understanding. Granted, many of the angelic names were loosely translated from their ancient Hebrew counterparts.

Either the authors pulled the angels' descriptions out of thin air (so to speak), or they actually saw and spoke to what they recorded. There's no clear cut yes/no in this and this does not mean everything recorded was a fundamental truism. My only argument has been to work from the book and see for yourself. Try it out as it is given and then make adjustments and record what you experience. In essence, this book is my attempt to do just that.

I doubt there is any black and white sense of "purism" in any magical art, but despite the scholarly inconsistencies and historical facts, the rituals of DSIC do work.

EXPERIENCING ANGELS IN THE CRYSTAL BALL

The appearances of the angels are, to me, secondary to the emotional impact of their arrival and notable signs of their presence. During operations, I have come to the understanding that if an angel is present (and desires you to be aware of its presence), you will notice a striking difference in the atmosphere, as well as in your emotions. Their arrival may be sudden or gradual, subtle or dynamic, but it will make a notable sign of its presence when a successful evocation is accomplished. This is important to remember, as you will not need to imagine anything for the successful working of this art. You may not have the strongest spiritual sight, but these entities will be noticeable when they are near, regardless. The marking of their presence is felt even after their departure. Being in the midst of such a spirit tends to leave you feeling exalted, yet humbled; a sense of holiness and power is felt within the space they occupied, and sometimes through the entire building or home. Likewise, you should notice a distinct contrast between your feelings before and after you began the operation. Although these Archangels can be intimidating and overwhelming at times, they should never leave you feeling depressed or horrified in anyway. Remember that they are called through the sacred ceremonies of magic with the protection and assistance of the Most High.

Their appearance is not quite like anything which can be imagined, and it is best to take them exactly as you perceive them, even if the vision of them is initially confusing. Don't bother trying to form an image in your imagination. Be patient and allow the vision to come naturally. Allow comprehension of what you see to come in its own time and avoid trying to force the vision to conform to your previous assumptions. I've found that the more open and free from mental distractions you are, the clearer your communication with the angel will be.

Vision within the crystal sphere is somewhat paradoxical and indefinable. At first, I likened it to viewing one of those 3D pictures where your eyes focus on a figure that seems to have no dimension, yet occupies the same space as your crystal ball. Whether or not this is similar to what other magicians experience, I cannot say. I speak only from personal experience. The visions of the angels who appear in the crystal sphere are usually beautiful and bright to behold, yet, at the same time, unnerving.

Signs of true angelic arrival can involve instances of increased light with no discernible source. You may perceive gold, violet, or electric blue colored specks in the air. You may experience the sensation of a powerful presence. The sound of a strong and clear voice projecting from thin air is an obvious indication, as is the lingering scent of flowers or other pleasant odors. All of these are all indicators of a holy or angelic presence. An angel's voice might be distinctly heard, but I've come to believe that they may not be speaking in ways we are used to. If you enter the operation with a clear mind and maintain it during the ritual, you may begin having impressions which will not seem to have originated from you; this is also a very possible form of angelic communication. During these times, you have to keep from talking over the angel by letting your mind remain open to receive clear communication. Ask your questions aloud or in your mind directly to the angel and then wait for the reply.

Although ethereal in nature and design, angels seem to have a defining presence of day and time. That is to say, they will appear best under certain days and times and will work best for you under those same specifications. This is alluded to in scripture, as well as widely elaborated upon in magical texts. Whether or not angelic beings are truly subject to the days, times, and the celestial movements of our physical planets, they seem to respond as if they are. If nothing else, these temporal correspondences may be meant to aid clearer communication or energetic channels between human and spirit. Spiritual denizens of unseen worlds have been placed into correspondence tables by magicians for centuries, and the seven planetary angels are no different.

For the most reliable correspondence charts concerning these angels, I recommend the webpage: *http://www.Archangelsandangels.com/aa_pages/ correspondences/Archangels_corresp_index.html.*

This will give you plenty of material to work with. Be prepared for what possible defining traits an angel will have, but do not allow yourself to be limited by what you have read. These beings are still beyond mankind's attempt to categorize them. Remember that each angel's most prominent time of rule is on the first and eighth hours of their day, and the third and tenth hours of the night. To find out your angel's time with relative ease, visit: *http://www.astrology.com.tr/planetary-hours.asp.*

Below are a few of the correspondences of each Archangel that are relevant to the experiment of DSIC. Included are my personal descriptions and reflections on each of these beings. Also, I have added the general call for each day found in *A Complete Book of Magic Science.* The calls should only be used after successful contact of the initial Archangels listed below. Studying all applicable symbols and related information will help to internalize the aspects of each angel or spirit. Keep in mind that only true interaction will give you a sense of what these powerful beings really contain.

Ruler of Saturday
Cassiel
קפציאל
"Speed of God"
Planet: Saturn
Other Known Names: Qafsiel, Captiel, Kafziel
Correct Pronunciation: cas-A-EL
Metal: Lead
Day: Saturday
Direction for Invocation: North

The appearance of this Archangel can be very unnerving at first encounter. Actually, his presence will likely unsettle you during most encounters. This was the first angel I evoked using this magical system and is the experience I relate in detail near the end of the book. He first appeared as a hooded figure with a pale face. He has since appeared as an old man with a beard and as a tall man with pale face and bald head. Dark, spiny wings jet out in numerous arrays from his shoulders. He is typically garbed in a dark black robe, carries a staff or scythe in one hand, and a book or "vessel" in the other. Sometimes, he is seen riding a dragon or pale horse. His demeanor is somber and intense, along with an eerie stillness that foretells of his presence. Regardless of the chilling sensation he initially gives, you may notice a clear centering effect he has on your psyche, clearing the mind of all distraction.

Beginning your operation with Cassiel, it is essential for clearing new space to help integrate the working of celestial influences within your lifestyle. The Archangel of Saturn is the guardian of the threshold that divides the material and spiritual worlds. This mighty Archangel will make room to begin incorporating the beneficial aspects of the spheres. Beginning with this spirit will most likely not bring phenomenal gifts of great celestial power, but he will entice both confrontation and consolidation of your inner being. It will take patience and determination to move past fears, aspirations, and doubts to reap the rewards this angel presents.

Cassiel brings forth what we hide from ourselves, as well as from others. He will bring to the surface aspects of ourselves kept hidden for far too long and allow them to be dealt with properly. Our fears represent lessons to be learned, but can become a storehouse of evil if left isolated and chained within the unconscious. Sometimes, we are afraid to let go or let certain aspects "die" or be removed from ourselves. Often, we are unable to let go of people, places, situations, or ideals we hold as important but are no longer useful or beneficial to have in our lives. If confronted with a stance of self-compassion, you will find a source of power and purpose you may have been completely unaware of. Moving past the fears of aging and death are among the most valuable gifts this angel can offer.

Cassiel is also able to assist with matters of the home, of foundation, and on the principles these establishments are set upon. This Archangel soberly understands the virtues or vices we carry with us into old age and that will continue to be worked through in further cycles of incarnation. Although he is of a far removed and celestial nature, Cassiel is the embodiment of earth, cultivation, and the working of the seasons of nature. It is remarkable to experience the paradoxical nature of this angel who embodies the deepest, darkest mysteries of the void and also the most solidified, natural aspects of physical reality. As opposite as they may seem, they are apparently two sides of the same coin. In establishing your life's purpose and long term goals, no other angel is best suited to help uncover the mystery of your being and give you a solid path. You may find through Cassiel that negative results in life stem from the ego's refusal to let go of outgrown fantasies and delusions.

General Invocation for the spirits of Saturday from *A Complete Book of Magic Science:*

> *Come out of your gloomy solitude ye Saturnine spirits, come with your cohort, come with diligence to the place where I am going to begin my operation under your auspices; be attentive to my labors and contribute your assistance that it may rebound to the honour and glory of the Highest.*

♃

SACHIEL

ᛉᚣᛁ

Ruler of Thursday
Sachiel
זכיאל
"Righteousness of God"
Planet: Jupiter
Other Known Names: Zachiel, Zedekiel, Zadakiel,
Tzadqiel (צדקיאל), Tzadkiel, Zedekul
Correct Pronunciation: Sach-EE-El
Metal: Tin, Brass, Bronze
Day: Thursday
Direction for Invocation: Southwest

The great Archangel of Jupiter, Sachiel, appears as a mighty king in long, flowing blue and purple robes. He first appeared to me as a strong elderly man with light shining from his brow. He had a sparkling crown upon his head, which seemed to be more of a solid halo. A large gold and blue scepter was held in his arm which flashed intermittently during the course of the operation. Often, I've see a large bird soaring behind him. He has a commanding voice and gestures powerfully while he speaks. Being in his presence is magnificent and awe inspiring. He is the visage of an energetic ruler whose gaze is wise and penetrating. I've evoked Sachiel the most in this art and appreciate the results from the experiences I've had. His Jovian aspect and generosity never cease to astound me. My achievement in this art and creation of the book you are now reading is largely in credit to him. My birth sign is ruled by his planetary authority and much of my other personal magic involves aspects of his nature.

All the mastery of your spiritual, emotional, and physical life is symbolized in the manifestation of his ruling. Listen to his council and advice without arrogance or self-deceiving justification. To be wise in the ruling of yourself, you must truthfully examine each action and intention critically, and be sure of their appropriateness for your intended goal. Health, wealth, and prosperity are the main benefits of working with this planetary Archangel. Learning to rule your own kingdom with wisdom and discernment are the true gifts of Sachiel. Any magic concerning abundance or the attainment thereof should be performed under this angel and on his day. Aspirations in the professions of law and politics are aided greatly by this Archangel, as well.

General Invocation for the spirits of Thursday from *A Complete Book of Magic Science:*

Come speedily ye blessed spirits who preside over the operation of this day. Come, Incomprehensible Zebarel and all your legions, haste to my assistance and be propitious to my undertakings, be kind and refuse me not your powerful aid and assistance.

⚷

SAMAEL

Ruler of Tuesday
Samael
סמאל
"Venom of God"
Planet: Mars
Other Known Names: Azazel, Sammael and Samil
Correct Pronunciation: sam-A-El
Metal: Bronze, Iron, Brass.
Day: Tuesday.
Direction for Invocation: South

Archangel Samael usually appears as an imposing male warrior, dressed in red and golden armor. His wings seem to constantly generate flames that travel the length of the large feathers, looking more like pulsing lights than wings. He has dark red hair and a severe expression. His eyes are penetrating and vigilant. In his right hand, he holds a wicked looking sword. In his left hand, he holds a shield hammered into the face of a screaming beast. There is a dark smoke that seems to constantly drift near his image and surroundings.

When you need the courage to overcome difficult obstacles or enemies, Samael is the angel to call to your aid. His arrival brings on an intense and almost challenging atmosphere. Very masculine and aggressive energy seems to fill the room at his coming. You must use caution when evoking this spirit to appear before you and always have a good reason to do so. Although very helpful in conquering any challenges, this angel seems to encourage discord and conflict in many situations. If your motivations or purpose for conjuring him are not lawful or ethical, he will challenge your reasoning. However, Samael can assist with competitions of any kind and will offer sound advice. Just having Samael in your presence will fill you with a desire for competition and striving against others to succeed at top performance. His encouragement could also assist you in any professional endeavors where you might be competing against other employees. You would want the strength of this angel before entering into battle or physical conflict of any kind. All matters dealing with war, challenge, violence, endurance, assertiveness, masculine sexuality, courage, and victory fall under this angel's banner. It is important to center yourself again after evoking this angel. Samael's intensity can be felt to linger in the air and may cause aggressive tendencies long after the ceremony's completion. Any anger that is stored in the psyche that has been brought on by feelings of inadequacy, guilt, or perceived harm by others may be disturbingly brought to the surface. I encourage caution when contacting this mighty being.

General Invocation for the spirits of Tuesday from *A Complete Book of Magic Science*:

Come military warlike Genii who have executed the order of the Sovereign Master of the Universe upon the armies of the rash Sennacherib, come and assist me in the operation that I undertake under the auspices of the third brilliant luminary of the firmament; be favorable to my entreaties in the Name of Adonay Sabaoth.

Ruler of Sunday
Michael
מִיכָאֵל / מיכאל
"He who is onto the likeness of God"
Planet: Sun
Other Known Names: Mîkha'el (Hebrew), Mikha'il (Greek)
Correct Pronunciation: Me-KAH-el
Metal: Gold, Brass
Day: Sunday
Direction for Invocation: West/South

Michael is the spirit mentioned in the example of DSIC text in *The Magus*. His sigil and name can be seen on the example lamen and magic circle on page 128. Michael is a mighty Archangel who appears as a shining figure, much like the sun itself. He is the model image of the gallant warrior, dressed in a bright yellow cloak and gold tunic. He carries a great sword in his right hand, which is held in commanding readiness. The light that issues from and around him is so intense that it is almost difficult to look at; the warmth of it can be felt through the crystal sphere. His commanding voice seems to echo and permeate throughout the entire chamber. Michael is the most divine protector, and holiness radiates from him into every corner of your magical chamber. No evil can withstand his presence.

Garnering the attention of the entire celestial host is achievable through Archangel Michael. I suggest asking for his blessing and authority to contact and communicate with all other spiritual beings. More than this, his gifts are divine protection, healing, and support. He is invoked in numerous occasions to keep unruly spirits in check. He is the General to the Most High, and retainer of the sanctity of Israel. Michael is able to dissolve all feelings of iniquity or spiritual injury. An intense joy and sense of renewal is felt after a successful invocation of him. You may notice how people are drawn to you after your operation. His light seems to imbue itself into your being and other people are often aware of it, if only on an unconscious level. When you need to shine or have the support of the divine with you, Michael is the Archangel to contact. Any action needing positive influence and charisma will be under his influence. He will help you in any sincere and honest endeavor, offering not only beneficial advice and council, but encouragement, which can only be described as divine assistance.

General Invocation for the spirits of Sunday from *A Complete Book of Magic Science:*

Come, Heavenly Spirits who hast the effulgent rays of the Sun. Luminous Spirits who are ready to obey the power of the great Tetragrammaton, come and assist me in the operation that I am making under the auspices of the Grand Light of Day which our Creator hath formed for the use of universal nature. I invoke you for these purposes. Be favorable and auspicious to what I shall ask in the Name of Amioram, Adonai Sabaoth.

Ruler of Friday
Anael
אָנָאֵל / ענאל
"Joy of God," "Grace of God"
Planet: Venus
Other Known Names: Anani, Ariel, Hamiel, Hanael, Hananel, Haniel,
Khananel, Onoel
Correct Pronunciation: An-A-EL
Metal: Copper or Brass
Day: Friday
Direction for Invocation: North

Anael first appeared to me in side profile. This was the first angel who appeared quite obviously female. Although I think gender is a relative term when used to describe an angel, this Archangel was quite definitely a woman in appearance and manner. Ironically, this goes counter to certain relations of Trithemius, but it is what I experienced. The angel looked as if she was standing upon the edge of a shoreline with rich green meadows directly behind and to the side. In her palm, she held a brilliant light which radiated throughout the entire crystal. The angel appeared lovely and intense at the same time. Her expression was indescribable as she turned to look at me. Her presence made me feel pleasant and nervous all at the same time. Graceful and beautiful, this angel comes dressed in layers of greenish silk beset by dark-reddish accents. Love, relationships, desires, and coming to terms with your innermost longings are the areas this angel understands most. By Anael, beauty in every definable area is crafted into the arts, sciences, and expressions of the human psyche. The desire to create, enjoy, and perceive the world around seems to be encouraged by this wondrous spirit.

Anael related to me the beautiful and creative patterns of countless actions in nature and humanity. She described true appeal to others as beginning with the unification and true acceptance of all aspects of their being, especially the parts we dislike. This unconditional acceptance of "the other" is a necessary part of *The Work*. Healing the heart from the hurt of past relationships and losses are all achievable through this spirit and should be embraced. By this angel's guidance, the understanding and acceptance of such experiences can be brought into clearer focus. It is important to not close off any aspects of your emotions while dealing with Anael. Although we would like to believe we are whole and unwavering magicians, the truth of the matter is that we are still fallible human beings. We all have hurts and pains that have been buried deep and for so long, we have almost forgotten they are there. Openness, humbleness, and sincerity will be your most powerful assets for truly integrating the "power" of this angel as well as all others. If pursued with openness, Anael will lead you to express your true talents in new and wondrous ways.

General Invocation for the spirits of Friday from *A Complete Book of Magic Science:*

Come on the wings of the wind, ye happy Genii who preside over the workings of the heart. Come in the Name of the Great Tetragrammaton; hear favorably the invocation that I make this day, destined to the wonder of love. Be ready to lend me your assistance to succeed in what I have undertaken under the hope that you will be favorable

Ruler of Wednesday
Raphael
רְפָאֵל,
"Healing power of God," "God heals"
Planet: Mercury
Other Known Names: Israfil (Islamic)
Correct Pronunciation: Raf-A-EL
Metal: Quicksilver, Cinnabar, Aluminum
Day: Wednesday
Direction for Invocation: Northeast

This angel appeared to me with bright silvery and yellow light streaming from behind him, as if he were standing in front of the first rays of dawn. The bright yellow and violet colors blended with a silver line across a heavenly horizon which illuminated this angel's majestic appearance. The entire crystal seemed haloed with this light. He looked to be wrapped in pale lemon yellow and light violet robes which folded together and unwrapped again as if blown by a breeze. An intricate staff was held in one hand, beset by scroll work, multi-colored stones, and images too numerous to count. A scroll of parchment with an endless array of letters, symbols and pictures was held in his other hand. The manuscript seemed to trail into infinite length behind him. His appearance is youthful and bright, with compassion and assurance being the truest expression on his face.

Archangel Raphael is a most benevolent and assisting angel. His presence brings instant balance and renewal. This angel will speak of wholeness coming with the integration and healing of past, present, and future. Communication, inspiration, and attainment of one's purpose are accomplished through the correct correlation between these experiences of man, according to him. Any dilemma may be overcome with this angel's assistance. If you are feeling stuck or in a place of stagnation, Raphael can help in getting things going again. The paradoxical nature of his counsel seems to be apparent when he encourages stability in one sentence and complete abandon in another. He explains that imbalance is needed to encourage change and growth, all in the correct amounts. This angel is an amazing problem solver and very clever in all aspects of human endeavor. He seems interested in the potential of humanity and sympathetic to the hurt which is caused by and to us. Anyone who successfully acquires his audience will be gifted with a new understanding and sense of vitality to carry out what they are meant to in this lifetime. According to Trithemius, Raphael is one of the seven angels of the Apocalypse (this opinion is derived from Enoch 20) and numbered among the ten Holy Sephiroth. His planetary role is often switched with Michael and can be found differing from what is given in the *Heptameron* versus the magical calendar. I have not encountered any difficulty with this apparent discrepancy, however.

General Invocation for the spirits of Wednesday from *A Complete Book of Magic Science:*

> *Run to me with speed, come to me ye Spirits who preside over the operation of this day, hear favorably the present invocation that I make to you under the Divine Names of Venoel, Uranel, be kind and ready to second my undertakings. Render them efficacious.*

Ruler of Monday
Gabriel
גַבְרִיאֵל
"Strength of God"
Planet: Moon
Other Known Names: Abruel, Gabrielus (Latin), Gavri'el
(Hebrew), Jibril or Jibrail (Arabic), Serafili.
Correct Pronunciation: gay- BREE-EL
Metal: Silver
Day: Monday
Direction for Invocation: West

Angel Gabriel appeared as a tall figure with long hair the mixed of dark and bright white. Deep set and blue eyes regarded me as if looking past my face into the depths of my being. Besides his eyes, little of his features could be discerned, as his entire face seemed to glow outward into a bright halo, which caused the crystal to shimmer. A long silver horn was held in one hand at his waist. The detail and intricacies of the instrument was unlike anything I have ever seen. A large silver bowl of shimmering liquid was at his feet and scenes of a changing landscape continued to reflect on the outside of its polished surface. Every once in a while, I could see a figure or face appear on the surface of the liquid. It would form only to disappear again. Gabriel's robes appeared a majestic blue and silver, with gold accents that seemed to trail on forever behind him. A bright night sky filled with stars larger and brighter than what can be seen on earth created the backdrop of this awe-inspiring being. The angel's voice sent pressured sensations from my forehead to the sides of my temples as he spoke.

Gabriel can instruct on how to interpret your dreams to better understand the beneficial voices of creation. In fact, the richness and depth of your dreams may take a more intense edge after working with him. He mentioned that the deeds, fears, and hopes of humanity were all heard by him and brought to the Father. Anyone wishing to ascend their spirit to the furthest heavens must not be afraid to be baptized in the deepest well. When I asked about the silver cauldron before him, he explained that the images were of my *hidden* being and could only be seen clearly when the liquid was perfectly still. There is a sense that the true mastery of magic and understanding of the heavenly spheres is by the mechanism of this angel's office. However, he is unwilling to simply handover the keys to the gates of the universe if it is more than one can stand.

Completing the initial ritual circuit with Gabriel is quite appropriate for this art. With the introduction to the previous Archangels complete, the support generated through the working of their spheres will greatly increase the ease of calling forth further spirits. In essence, the real beginning starts with Gabriel and the moon after initial introductions are completed. All of the spheres are accessed through the celestial corridor of the Moon or *Yesod*. Gabriel is the Archangel of this gateway, the divine messenger between the world of form and the spiritual realm. Through him, the communication between all the previous spheres and his own can be accomplished. It may be interesting to note that the *crystal sphere*, which is used to descry these beings, is listed as the stone attributed to Gabriel in the *Three Books of Occult Philosophy* by Cornelius Agrippa.

General Invocation for the spirits of Monday from *A Complete Book of Magic Science:*

> *Haste ye Sublime and Subliminary Genii who are obedient to the Sovereign Arcana, come and assist me in the operation that I undertake under the auspices of the Grand Luminary of the Night. I invoke you to thus purpose be favorable and hear my entireties in the Name of Him Who commands the spirits who are Superiors in the Legions that you inhabit. Bileth, Mizabu, Abinzaaba.*

The above descriptions and illustrations should give you ample knowledge and references to form the correct links to each of the planetary angels. I presented each angel with their illustration, sigil or sign, along with important corresponding attributes which will be used in their evocation. Before any experiment of conjuration is undertaken, you should spend as much time as possible researching and familiarizing yourself with the being you are attempting to contact. Read and research for any biblical or occult lore that may exist on them. Familiarize yourself with their corresponding symbols and offices. The more you know, the better chance you will have on contacting the correct being, and you will also know which appropriate questions may be asked.

Continuing on with your experiments and future operations is imperative after this point, since the first cycle will have been more of an initiation process. You will have just scratched the surface of the true art of DSIC at this level. After completion of the first seven invocations, you should have a sense of what the seven planetary Archangels are about. Now, you can set about integrating their frequencies more potently within your life. Also, you are able to conjure their associated spirits for further assistance with any related situation.

I would not recommend evoking planetary demons until you feel you've balanced the associated spheres' correspondences completely within yourself. This is achieved naturally through a pure and open communication with the initial Archangels. A relationship is first established and then, through their authority, such chaotic beings as demons can be constructively petitioned. Again, if your ritual was conducted successfully, you will not have to imagine or force any of this. You will intrinsically be aware of the new frequencies within you.

Since writing this and sharing it with a few select students, I have responded to difficulties that arrive in the development of spiritual sight and hearing and the interaction with spiritual beings. Here is something that I told one of my students:

"I understand your concern with the scrying exercises and frustration with being unable to see clearer images in your stone. It does take a while and it's a paradoxical process of 'determined practice' and initial 'complete abandonment of expectation of the outcomes.' What I mean by that is, in essence, you are trying to see spirits and angels, but, at the same time, remain open and unattached to the outcomes. The Angels will appear and speak to you as they will and according to the understanding and comprehensions of your own mind. Remember that spiritual beings, as well as spiritual energy, don't look like anything in their own right — there is no need for them to. When we behold spirits, we are viewing the interpretation that our senses (mind) are giving us. Everything is symbolically expressed in this world through interpreted images, senses, sounds, and smells, which relate messages that are untranslatable in simple words.

"You mentioned before your experiences and interactions with Archangel Raphael and Gabriel, I believe, during some of your earlier scrying sessions. You seemed pretty sure of their presence and interaction. Don't downplay this or let the rational, logical mind try to convince you out of things, which it will try to do. Let it be what it is and stay with it; remain open.

"When you scry and call forth the angels under the DSIC ceremony, things will occur that won't seem 'by the book' or expected and you have to not let this shake you. In one of my evocations, the spirit didn't just appear in the crystal; it filled up the whole gold disk. Another time, I forgot about the crystal pedestal altogether and just found myself looking upon a full sized apparition, but I was completely unsure if I was even gazing in the crystal's direction at that time. I've even forgotten about my wand, my circle, and almost the whole ceremony during one of the more intense conversations and visions of the angels, and it was perfectly fine.

"As magicians, we may sometimes find ourselves walking the nebulous path of the mystic, who does nothing to control or placate spiritual interactions. We try to control, record, and examine the effects of our mystical undertakings and experiences, but they are rarely cut and dry. It really is an art form, as if we are binding two separate entities together in hopes of attaining some level of understanding of the non-physical. We have to train our minds to not compare our experiences to other's experiences — not mine or anyone else's. We should not have expectations of how things 'should be.' The whole trick to altered awareness, scrying, and ascendant consciousness is knowing that space where your imagination is not 'making things up' and the impressions you receive are not analyzed or judged, but are allowed to flow naturally and at their own frequency.

"The above reasons are why you should not try to summon anything forth yet. All the greatest seers and clairvoyants never forced their abilities to exist or manifest; they worked at their own accord. From your correspondence, I'm fairly confident you are on the right track and making those connections which are needed to continue. It's easy to doubt and second guess ourselves. The angels and spirits are real, but never quite what we think they are.

"Once you finally stand in your circle and the implements you worked so hard to create are being set to the course and purpose of their design and your mind has integrated the details of the ceremony, the corresponding energies will align naturally and bring forth the intended spirit. Your comprehension/apprehension of them will be dictated by your state of being, awareness, and openness to them. Save your analysis, reflection, and logical processing to well after the rite has been concluded."

If the prospect of contacting these beings stirs something within you, yet you are doubtful of your ability to see them, you may consider asking for assistance. It is very difficult to conduct a ritualized ceremony and maintain the correct mindset while attempting to view and communicate with spirits at the same time. Historically, communing with angels and spirits was rarely done alone. If we are to go by many of the classical works of ritual magic, most evocations were done with at least one other attending assistant. Often, a magician would use a scryer (one who can descry or "see" spirits) to relate what he saw and heard from the spirits, while the magician could concentrate on recording and asking further questions. In the next chapter, we will be exploring the very delicate task of working with a partner in sacred magic.

CHAPTER III

PARTNERS IN MAGIC

any modern authorities of grimoric magic frown upon having anyone else present during experiments of Evocation or Invocation. Their arguments are only valid in face of the possible dilemmas that another person might present. The main issue I have with these writers is that this is *not* the tone of most classical texts of magic. In fact, some grimoires mention that someone should always be present with you during magical rituals of evocation. The Trithemius experiment is one such text: *"Note: In these dealings, two should always be present, for often a spirit is manifest to one in the crystal when the other cannot perceive him…"*

Group workings in ritual evocation were more the rule rather than the exception in the classic period of magic. Despite any problems one might have with a shifty scryer, there could also be issues of ego and ownership for magical discoveries on the part of the magician. Unfortunately, humility and humbleness are virtues found lacking in many modern magicians.

Keep all avenues open for communication with divine messengers, avoiding the willful presumptions that stunt further spiritual encounters. You might recall that in the Holy Magic of Abramelin, the mage, a young boy-assistant, sees and is able to look upon the magician's Holy Guardian Angel (HGA) long before the magician himself is allowed to look upon him. There is no reason to be abashed for having a respectable partner assist you in your magical endeavors of evocation.

FINDING A SCRYER

In your searching to become familiar with the plethora of spiritual beings which inhabit the world and integrating spheres, you might come across a gifted person who, for some reason or another, has the ability to see beyond the veil of the physical. Even if you have developed your astral sight, be open to the possibility of someone having slightly better eyes than yourself. Chance encounters with such an individual should be taken as a possible sign that the divine is steering you toward a beneficial magical relationship. Take nothing for granted, however, and use your intuition and discretion to be sure of the person's character and how they would complement your work. Such an individual needn't be an expert in the same magical field of study as you, nor understand the fine principles of magic.

A beneficial scryer might be someone who has had "experiences" most or all of their life. They might not be in full understanding of how it works, or even eager to disclose such experiences to just anyone. Conversations of this sort should always be handled carefully and with due respect.

Be sure to choose a person of honest character and talent. An experimental trial run with your scryer might finalize your decision to use or move on from that particular working relationship. As the magician/operator, you should be able to determine your scryer's credibility from their body language, tone of voice, related information, and honest reply to your questions. If responses seem a bit too scripted or fantastical, you may have a charlatan on your hands and should immediately dismiss him or her from your magical experiments.

Despite the stereotype, I am convinced of an angel's appreciation for people who are generous, respectable, self-controlled, and truthful. If the possible scryer is interested in assisting you, an interview process much like a high-level corporate position might be appropriate. Consider ahead of time which questions you would ask, what you would require, and how you would keep the shared information between the two of you. It does not matter if the person is a longtime friend, family member, or new acquaintance. There should be an established code of mutual respect between you and your scryer at all times. Getting along with other people for lengths of time can be a challenge for many of us and getting along with someone who shares in the intimate workings of the Great Art can add stress exponentially.

The person who is to become your seer should be sensitive to your goals and sympathetic to your work. Women are typically more intuitive than men and can be exceptionally talented scryers. The role of women, as scryers, has arguably received too little credit in the records of medieval magic. No doubt this was due to the strict fraternal nature of the monasteries at those times (unless you include nunneries, which were not privy to the same educational materials). Women seers often assisted in magical operations, but such recorded accounts are scarce, due to the fanatical witch executions which lasted for hundreds of years throughout Europe. Sometimes, the bonds of close relationships strengthen rather than distract from magical operations. This is a factor each magician must honestly determine for themselves. Many magician–scryer couples are, or have become involved in, an intimate relationship after sharing magical experiments.

A prime example of a working, modern magus–scryer relationship would be Magus and author Aaron Leitch and his wife, Carrie Mikell. They are a couple of complementary talents, who by their accounts work fantastically well together in traditional conjurations of spirits. To read more about their experiences and amazing accounts to Solomonic requests and workings, see Mr. Leitche's accounts on his *Ananael Blog* at: http://aaronleitch. wordpress.com/tag/aaron-leitch/.

WORKING WITH A SCRYER

Below, I will discuss tips for working with a person you have chosen as your scryer. My frame of reference comes from my years of practicing as a hypnotherapist, working with clients, close friends, and family members. I will be comparing two situations which do not necessarily correlate with one another at first glance. I choose this example to illustrate a point and offer ideas of beneficial working between magus and seer. In working with clients under hypnosis, there are noticeable dissimilarities between someone simply in a trance and someone involved in communicating with an entity. Although both situations may involve altered states of consciousness, one is geared toward the hidden-internal, while the other is focused on the hidden-external. Determining where this boundary exists is the preoccupation of the physical mind. I use the knowledge that the spirits bequeath to me and I leave cyclical debates alone.

In hypnotherapy sessions where the client is coming to the hypnotherapist/hypnotist for personal reasons rather than for entertainment, the person filling the role of hypnotist has many ethical obligations. Foremost, it is their goal to guide the client into relaxed states of thought that promote a heightened awareness in the particular area of the mind they are trying to access. The hypnotherapist must be cautious not to willfully or unconsciously push the subject into experiencing or believing something they want them to believe. This technique is referred to as implanting suggestions or "leading." The hypnotist must also know how to read the states of consciousness of the subject and know how and when to ask appropriate questions or request certain things.

During the DSIC operation, the interrogative questions are just as much for the spirit as they are for the scryer. This equally applies to you, regardless of whether you are the scryer or the magus. The ordered dialog keeps the session from becoming random or chaotic. Spiritual beings, as well as the information they present, do not typically relate in a linear or organized fashion. As such, open ended questions or inquiries may lead the magician into spirals of seemingly disjointed responses and confusing tangents. The interrogation outline will be explained in the "Steps for Evocation" section of this book. The questions which Trithemius gives are designed to garner what pertinent information is applicable for the purpose of the ritual.

In my experience, spirits, whether angelic or goetic, either dislike idle chit chat with human beings or enjoy talking yarns of ceaseless tangents. Just as it is important for the hypnotist to guide the session toward its proper conclusion, so too is it the magician's responsibly to control the session between person(s) and spirit until the close of the ritual. The magician should have all questions considered and written down ahead of time. Avoid mundane discussions of trivial matters. Consider using polite diplomacy as your method of verbal communication to guard against distracting tangents. Be patient with yourself and your scryer and take the time you would allow yourself to interact between nobility from a different country. Remember, successful contact and appearance of a spiritual being does not imply successful interaction with them.

The scryer acts as an intermediary and the magus has to rely on their account to know how the dialog is progressing. It is important to give time between requests to allow the scryer to absorb all that the spirit is saying or doing. You do not want to rush or question your scryer prematurely, as it may interrupt the entire dialog. A hypnotized subject, like a person in deep trance, will explain things to the best of their comprehensive abilities. Many things in the deep unconscious, as well as the spiritual or astral worlds, seem confusing to the conscious, rational mind. Symbolic representation is the primary mode of communication in the unseen worlds.

Be sure to record all information as it is related to you. Ask only important and relevant questions. Be patient, but be involved, and set the pace for the operation. When your operation is drawing to a close, allow a moment for your scryer to regain their state of wakeful consciousness. Record everything down to the closing prayer. Afterwards, take a few breaths, and discuss the results of the operation between yourself and your scryer. This will help to procure a fuller picture of what has transpired.

The vast majority of my magical operations and especially evocations of spirits has been done solo, which has seemed to be the preferred method of modern occultists despite the many classical writings pointing to the contrary. However, within the past few years I have had the great fortune to practice the art of angelic conjuration with a fellow magician and long standing friend, and we work excellently together. He is someone I had always respected greatly and who had impeccable integrity and discernment for what was real and what was fantasy. He was also highly motivated and disciplined, practicing his magical rituals and meditations on a daily basis despite any amount of inconvenience or health troubles. I knew him to be tremendously gifted in receiving prophetic dreams, visions, and contacts with spiritual beings. He eagerly volunteered to join me in my magical endeavors.

Our first experiments involved methods of astral projection or soul travel and scrying/traveling to the elemental planes using *Tattva* cards. Originating from the Samkhya version of Hindu Philosophy, Tattva scrying was a practice developed by the Hermetic Order of the Golden Dawn to experience the astral dynamism of the five elements of creation. The main cards consist of five shapes, each with one or two colors that "flash" and draw the eye. I had worked with the cards for several years but had never tried the practice with anyone else before.

The initial experiment was an exciting proposal for me to share practices I had delved into during the earlier parts of my magical training. My early foundation for ritual/ceremonial magic was based upon the principles found in the Golden Dawn, and it was fascinating to discover just how much my ability and methods had matured over the years. In this sense, the practices, as well as my magical tools, have undergone quite a metamorphosis to encompass my understanding and experience.

I found that hypnosis used with the added efforts of the magician's *Will* to draw others into a shared mystical experience to be an invaluable tool.

I realized that if I can just "get the person there," the rest of the ceremony will follow suit without me having to paint a picture of what the experience "should" look like. The scryer beholds what they will all on their own and with their own perceptions. The flow of the ceremony should produce the feeling of "otherness" in the atmosphere regardless. Hypnosis is effective, but not necessary if the scryer is able to get themselves into the proper mindset by themselves.

The experiences of working with a scryer have been extremely rewarding with additional input and feedback that comes from having a second observer. We have continued to work together and have vastly enjoyed the results and benefits of each magical operation.

Even if the idea of working with another person seems undesirable to you, I encourage you to be open to the possibility. For many of us, myself included, no such partner was initially presented, so I worked alone to the best of my ability. If you are determined to work alone or simply cannot find a suitable partner, there is hope. The *proper* practice of magic itself will help one to become attuned to the subtle energies around him or her. Determination and persistence in this art will allow the sincere magician to become more aware and sensitive to the non-physical world.

There are numerous books for developing and honing the ability to scry or perceive spirits. Some are helpful where others are not worth your while. A point to keep in mind is that classical or grimoric magicians prayed, meditated, and fasted to be granted the ability to perceive spirits. (Refer to the Ars Notoria prayers of *Lemegeton*) Modern magicians may utilize some of these methods, but also perform visualizations and rituals to increase their *sight* and perceptions. It seems as if modern magic is geared more toward the person developing their own abilities, while the grimoires insist that such abilities are received from God. When done with pure and proper intention, both methods can be utilized toward successful ends. In the next chapter I offer the practices I've found to be most beneficial for developing the ability to see spirits.

CHAPTER IV

PREPARATION FOR SCRYING

n DSIC, as well as most grimoires which deal with crystal gazing, there is an assumption that one already has at least some ability to descry the presence of spirits. Many authors have taken it upon themselves to instruct the neophyte magician in this art of seeing images in a mirror or stone. Despite the wide range of knowledge available and how-to books, I find that very few ceremonial magicians are actually competent in this field. Unsurprisingly, the two main causes for this problem explain the reason.

First, few people actually have a natural aptitude for perceiving spiritual phenomena in the first place. New Age books and popular television programs on the supernatural lead many to believe that just about everyone has the ability to see spirits if they just bother to stare at something in a darkened room long enough. Unfortunately, this is not the case and many initially excited seekers become disheartened and fizzle out after their practices failed to yield the results they had hoped for. Secondly, few westerners in this day and age have the patience and persistence necessary to hone an ability which, at first, seems unrewarding.

I consider myself lucky to have had a time in my life where I lived alone and was determined to be able to experience this effect without a multitude of distractions or preoccupations. I had already mastered some methods for putting myself into a meditative or hypnotic state where I could focus my mind on one point for an extended period of time. I recall my first successful scrying exercise where I saw a large bird or eagle flying in side profile. It appeared clearly like I was watching it on TV, but with a photographic negative or diffused glowing effect. I remember sitting and starring at this phenomena for a while, as it was one of the first moving images I recall being able to see and which would still be there after I had looked away and back again.

The second thing that stood out during this particular scrying exercise was the appearance of my grandmother. She had passed away months earlier, but suddenly appeared in my peripheral vision rather than in the mirror or in a defined "space." She looked younger than I had known her, but she was easily recognizable and I knew her at once. She spoke to me about some concerns she had about my father, who was having difficulty with her passing. She wished for me to tell him of the ease of her passing and other information that was personal to my family.

After this profound experience, I practiced my scrying more often than before. I would just sit in front of the mirror, letting whatever images that wished appear to do so without conscious effort or expectation. Luckily, I never witnessed anything horrifying or grotesque in the mirror — just shapes and colors swirling, faces of people I did not recognize, and various landscapes and sceneries that did not seem to have any discernible meaning, at first. As I continued with this work, I soon began educating myself on the practices of the grimoires and the intentional evocation of certain spirits.

The system of magical ritual we will be working from utilizes a crystal sphere for the viewing of the aforementioned Archangels in the previous chapter. The crystal is the focal point of the operation and the object which acts as the communication device between the magician (or scryer) and the angel. Being able to successfully scry a crystal sphere is essential for this art. The practice described below, however, is meant to greatly improve your aptitude and consistency in scrying any medium.

The black mirror was what I started with when I began practicing the art of scrying. The wide viewing surface seemed to help block out peripheral distractions and draw my gaze. The very nature of its dark, depthless surface naturally causes the eyes to focus past the physical surface of the glass. Although a crystal ball is closer to what is required for the practice of DSIC, both the dark mirror and crystal sphere are viable scrying tools. For the beginner to amateur scryer, I suggest practicing with a black mirror, as it seems easier to use for extended periods of time.

I practiced scrying every week, sometimes nightly, just to see what would show up in the black mirror in my darkened room. After nearly two years of fairly consistent practice, I diverted my attention from attempting to see spirits in the black mirror to trying to perceive them in three-dimensional space. I became enraptured by the idea of traditional evocation without the use of a scrying medium. Although I may have ceased my scrying practices a bit prematurely, I valued the experiences immensely and eventually resumed them with the undertaking of the *Art Almadel* of *Lemegeton*.

I conducted a full year's cycle of evoking each of the seasonal angels of the *Art Almadel* every Sunday. The experiments yielded major breakthroughs in spirit communication for me and eventually led to my success in being able to see and communicate with the angels of DSIC. Their appearances and interactions were clearer than anything I had ever witnessed before within a crystal ball. Somehow my perceptions were allowed to fully behold what the grimoires alluded to and which I had always secretly hoped existed but had never been truly convinced of till that moment.

As with the majority of this work, I share what I have experienced myself or learned through study of the grimoires, but I do not claim to know what methods will work for each person. For those interested and wishing to increase their abilities with viewing the angelic beings of the DSIC system, I can only suggest what I have undergone to develop my own spiritual sight. It is truly my hope that you will experience the same wonders I have.

First, I would recommend you purchase and/or make a few implements to act as your *practice* scrying equipment. With these items, no elaborate consecration ceremonies will need to be conducted, nor will the equipment be all that difficult to find or construct. The exercises and experiences gained by following the methods below will undoubtedly assist you in becoming competent in *The Art of Drawing Spirits into Crystals*.

To begin, I would suggest obtaining a large crystal sphere, dark scrying mirror, obsidian sphere, or, if you're a wealthy mage, you can buy a large, polished, obsidian mirror. If, for some reason, you are unable to do any of the above, you can try making your own scrying mirror, which is actually quite easy to do and my preferred method.

You can create a dark scrying mirror in a variety of ways using a few simple techniques. I suggest getting into the habit of working during favorable astrological times in order to become attuned to them. You might try to purchase or begin making your scrying equipment while observing a favorable lunar day (Monday), time, and alignment. The moon should also be waxing or increasing in light. For seeing spirits, *Veritable Key of Solomon* declares that the Moon and Mercury are both beneficial. Refer to an astrological almanac to see if the Moon and Mercury are in agreement or at least not apposing in any way before you begin working. If possible, the Moon should also be in an earth sign. An ideal time to create or purchase your scrying mirror or orb would be on a Monday, during an hour of a Moon or Mercury while it is in the sign of Capricorn, Taurus, or Virgo.

If you wish to construct your own scrying mirror, the first task will be to find or have a piece of round glass cut at a glass or hobby store. The thickness of the glass is relatively unimportant, but I suggest going with a large circle of anywhere between twelve to eighteen inches in diameter. The larger surface will help greatly, as you will be less likely to let your eyes drift off to objects or spaces behind or to the sides of the mirror.

If you decide to start your practices using a crystal sphere, I recommend selecting a fairly large one for the same reasons I listed above. You should choose one that is either perfectly clear or is at least free from any clouds, specks, or cracks which will confuse the mind into seeing something that isn't really there. You will need a suitable stand to hold your crystal or glass ball steady. There are many variations to choose from which are fairly inexpensive, and you will not need anything fancy or elaborate. Just be sure that your crystal does not reflect back any distracting optical illusions from the stand which will not benefit your scrying exercises.

If choosing the dark mirror, the second thing will be to paint it black on one side. Lay your glass flat on a soft surface that you don't mind getting paint on, but will also protect the glass and keep it from getting scratched. Next, apply several coats of black paint. I suggest using spray paint as it is less likely to smear and dries faster. Flat black is the traditional color to use, but glossy black, midnight blue or even deep indigo blue work very well also. A deep, dark blue can mimic the deep spiritual void or spiritual world quite well. I rather enjoy the indigo scrying mirror I made years back and use it to this day.

After you have added several coats to one side of your mirror, hold it up to a light source to be sure no spots have been missed. I would avoid using the sun for this however and instead use artificial or candle light and keep it out of the sun's rays. Keep it wrapped in a dark cloth to prevent it from being scratched, damaged, or carelessly handled by other people.

Another method for obtaining a scrying mirror is to purchase a piece of glass which is already tinted. One of the best scrying mirrors I ever worked with was one I had cut for me from a stained glass store. I bought a piece of dark black glass that had a smooth, undulating texture to it. I had it cut to a nine-inch diameter circle and waited for the full moon to consecrate it, using a conductive lunar mixture I concocted. I give the ingredients and procedures I used in this experiment below. I think the dark mirror worked best for me initially because it was often difficult to determine where the surface of the mirror was and it became hypnotically pulling. It was easy for my eyes to be drawn into the mirror's seemingly depthless surface.

CREATION AND USE OF THE FLUID CONDENSER

The term "fluid condenser" was popularized by the famous period magician, Franz Bardon, who authored *Introduction to Hermetics, The Practice of Magical Evocation* and many other works. This fluid is applied to the surface of the mirror or crystal sphere to imbue or "impregnate" it with a specific energy or to draw various sigils and symbols upon it for use in ritual. After using a fluid condenser on a mirror or crystal, be sure the mirror is cleaned and the surface protected before storing it away again.

To create a fluid condenser, you will first need to gather a few herbs and ingredients. Any herbs or plants that are used for your condenser should be freshly cut if possible. The magician at http://www.alchemy-works.com/ has a great selection of fresh herbs and mixtures ready to order. The lists of herbs below are all applicable to the art of seeing spirits, but do not need to all be included to make a good condenser. Only use the ones you can find that are of good quality. I would also recommend purchasing some new ceramic bowls and a small metal pot to be used for blending the ingredients together.

Ingredients for lunar conductive fluid condenser based on Veritable Key of Solomon:

- A two-ounce base of white sandalwood powder
- An ounce of orris root and myrrh in equal parts
- A half ounce of jasmine flowers (optional)
- One dried skin of a frog
- A small pinch of refined camphor
- A half ounce of white poppy seeds
- Small amounts of moonstone and silver dust shavings (extra adage)

- One dram of virgin olive oil
- A liter of distilled stream or rain water
- Two drams wood or isopropyl alcohol

Mix the white sandalwood, myrrh and orris root, and grind them together into a fine powder. True refined camphor can be difficult to come by, but if you should find some, add a pinch to the powdered base. Also, add in the poppy seeds and, if procured appropriately, skin of a frog. Put this mixture in an air-tight jar and let it sit in until the next full moon. On the evening of the next full moon, mix all the ingredients together with two drams of virgin olive oil in a silver or crystal bowl, if possible. Do all this while meditating on the purpose for the condenser which is assisting you with scrying into the spirit world. Recite this prayer of intention for added potency as you complete the above step:

"Dominus sorspartir, etcalieismei, tusustententabissortemmeam. Funescecideruntmihi in jucundia, insuperhaereditaspraeclaramihi."

Once you complete the above step, place the mixture in a pot with distilled water or rainwater. There should be about an ounce of each herb and enough water in the pot to cover the contents completely. Bring this mixture to a boil, and then let it simmer for an hour with the pot lid on. When this is done, let the mixture cool and strain it through an unbleached coffee filter or fine linen. Put the liquid back into the pot and allow it to simmer without the lid until only a quarter of the original amount is left. When this is cool, add small amounts of the fine silver shavings if you have any. Then, add the shavings of moonstone, again if you have them. When you have completed the above steps and allowed the mixture to cool, add an equal amount of wood or isopropyl alcohol to act as a preservative and poor the entire concoction into an air-tight bottle with a firm lid. Store the completed fluid condenser in a dark, cool location.

Incense is a traditional component that is used in practically every operation of ceremonial magic and is included in the DSIC experiment proper. It is not essential for the practice of scrying, but I offer it as an option to assist you in developing your astral sight. Traditional corresponding Lunar or Mercury incense blends are most appropriate for this practice and can aid one to enter the proper frame of mind. The Lunar incense mixtures, in particular, contain corresponding ingredients which are agreeable to the sphere of Yesod and harmonious with the fluid condenser described above. The incense used during your sessions should be soothing to your senses and not distracting in any way. Keep this in mind, as you will not require large amounts of smoke to be produced which could irritate the lungs and eyes. Your scrying incenses should also be blended together by hand, if possible, and burned on bits of charcoal in a fire-safe container. If you would like to experiment beyond using instant-light charcoal types, coals made from olive wood pieces are excellent for this type of practice.

Scrying incense blend:

- A base containing a full ounce each of mastic gum, myrrh, galangal powder, and frankincense
- An ounce each of mugwort and wormwood herbs
- A half ounce of rose petals and lavender buds
- Three green cardamom pods and star anise
- Three bay leaves
- Oils of mimosa and lotus, and dark musk

Blend together mastic, myrrh, galangal, and frankincense in equal parts, and grind all to a powder base. Add a few cardamom and star anise seeds to the base and place these in an air-tight jar. Now, mix equal parts of ground mugwort, wormwood, and bay leaves — about half the amount used in the powder base. Coat this mixture with dark musk oil and put it aside in a sealed jar. Mix the lavender and rose petals together, coat them with mimosa and lotus oil, and put them aside in another sealed jar. Let the ingredients stand for nine days during the waxing of the moon.

On the ninth evening, remove the anise and cardamom seeds from the first incense blend and discard; their scent will have been absorbed by the other ingredients. Then, blend all mixtures together by hand. The scrying incense is now ready and should be stored in an air-tight bottle as well. Use this particular incense for your scrying exercises only. This mixture has spectacular effects which cause the inner senses to awaken and form a link between the scryer and spiritual world. I have found that continued use of this particular incense has many beneficial qualities.

Important points for working with the black scrying mirror or crystal stone:

Always keep your scrying crystal, or mirror clean and free of smudges, smears and substances that could scratch the surface. Carefully wipe down the surface of your mirror or crystal after each use with a clean linen cloth.

Never use your scrying apparatus for anything but its intended purpose.

Do not let others idly look at or handle your scrying equipment. Keep your mirror or crystal wrapped in a black silk or linen cloth when not in use.

You may want to continue to practice the procedures described below until clear images begin appearing on a consistent basis.

Keep the working area clean and free from any mundane activity or items which do not belong.

For the first month or so, you may want to only scry at night, preferably during a waxing moon, depending on time availability. Scrying may be effective during day or night, but tends to work better during the evening hours.

If you wish to create a sanctified space to work in, first construct a circle using calk, white rope, or some other material. Eventually, we will be making one in the DSIC tradition described in *The Magus*.

Keep a journal to record each of your experiences, including the date, time, and astrological alignments.

I recommend beginning your scrying exercises in the evenings where outside noises and distractions are down to a minimum and sunlight will not be an issue. Eventually, you'll want to experiment in the day, as well as the evening, but for now, evening exercises are ideal. To further your magical attunements, choose an evening hour related to Mercury or the Moon. These are great times to explore and train your magical senses. Sessions should not extend past an hour and should be at least twenty to thirty minutes from beginning to end.

Your practices will be conducted while sitting upright in a chair since the DSIC operation is also done in this fashion. Another purpose for these exercises is to become familiar with the steps for setting up your scrying area and entering a receptive mental state without the extra demands placed upon you by the complete DSIC ceremony. You should attempt to build a consistent practice, regardless of results, making adjustments only as necessary to allow sessions to flow comfortably and with ease.

There are methods to scrying which require patience and determination. Unless you are accustomed to spending long periods of time focusing in meditative states, it will take time and effort to achieve the correct level of concentration needed for this art. Practice and experience will be imperative for discovering how to achieve the proper posture, focus, and gaze in order to connect your senses to the astral. This really took some time for me, and many nights were spent in frustration as I battled stiff muscles, distracting thoughts, and candles and incense not cooperating.

There are countless books on meditation and crystal/mirror gazing, so I was a bit hesitant about including another how-to portion that has been painfully overdone. However, I realize many magicians will be coming at this art from a fresher perspective and may also be interested in the methods I used to develop my own scrying abilities. To be fair, I learned many of these techniques from other occult works and have those authors and their works to thank for their willingness to share their knowledge. There is no book, however, that is going to *give* you a perfect method that will automatically produce results. If they happen to, it's because you were already a highly gifted seer to begin with. The rest of us need to work at it, constantly and tenaciously.

Continual involvement and active participation in these exercises will make bridging the gaps between the worlds that much more effective. However, this is a time consuming discipline that demands attention. It can cause juggling normal concerns of day-to-day life even more challenging than before.

Scrying chamber setup:

For both the crystal and dark mirror, a stand of some sort will be required to place them upon. Both the stand and scrying implement should be placed on a table that is large enough not to be knocked over if bumped, but light enough so it can be moved around the room. The table on which your scrying device rests should also be large enough to allow the candles to be placed on either side of your mirror or crystal. The type of candlesticks and candles are not important, but traditional white, black, or silver candles are appropriate colors for this work. I am a huge fan of pure beeswax candles, which I use in grimoric magical rituals of all sorts. They give off a very pleasant aroma and dispense positive ions into your working space. However, paraffin candles work just as well and any soft, natural light will suffice. When the candles are lit, remember to keep anything from reflecting directly off the crystal or mirror's surface. The mirror should appear as a dark tunnel or window to the spiritual void, and the crystal should give off a slight iridescent glow. Set up the mirror at eye level while sitting and set the two candles on either side far enough away so that no reflections of the flames appear on the mirror.

Also, a small incense burner and coals can be utilized and practiced with since this will also be an included element in the DSIC operation. There will be a list of appropriate incenses to practice with below to encourage the development of your visions.

As straightforward as this arrangement seems, these items take a bit of practice and experience to work with before they become a contribution to your scrying experience and not a distraction. Not only will you be practicing the art of scrying and attempting to view images in a mirror or stone, you will also be learning how to arrange and handle some of the basic components of the DSIC operation. The entire procedure may seem a bit time consuming at first, but as you make it a routine practice, you will discover how the arrangement, storage, and set up of all your magical equipment flows with ease.

You can form a small, protective circle in your scrying room if you chose. The circle for this exercise does not have to be a certain diameter, just large enough to encompass your sitting area. It can be constructed with chalk if you are working on concrete or a hard floor of some type. Rope, cloth, or any natural material will work. I've heard of some magicians using tape or other modern materials, but I would urge you to stick with mediums comparable to the ones you will be using in the DSIC operation. Reasonable creativity and simplicity are granted here for the sake of initiatory practice and since the object is to not contact any specific spiritual beings. Offer initiatory prayers, if you so you choose. *Key of Solomon* and *Lemegeton* (Ars-Notoria) both have "blessing prayers for place of working," which work well.

More appropriately, DSIC has a short prayer for blessing the magical working space which is to be used in the main operation. You can find the complete prayer in the "Putting it to Practice" section in this book. It would be wise to become familiar with this prayer and learn to recite it with authority.

For seeing spirits, *Veritable Key of Solomon* suggests that experiments should be conducted when the Moon is in in an earth sign. If you wish to consecrate your working space before you use it, you can incense the area with benzoin gum and sprinkle holy water around the perimeter. Do this on a Monday or Wednesday and during a time when the moon is waxing and in Capricorn, Taurus ,or Virgo. You can use benzoin incense and holy water to also bless your circle, tools, and the mirror or stone.

When you are ready to begin your scrying practice, start by washing your hands and face with clean water before walking into your magical room or working space. Enter without shoes and bring a small lit candle or lamp. Shut the door and make sure all outside light and distractions are closed out. Set your chair in the center of your circle and in front of your table with the scrying device and candles upon it. Before you light the candles on your table, begin by taking some deep breaths and speaking a prayer of intention, such as this opening prayer from *Key of Solomon:*

"O LORD God, Holy Father, Almighty and Merciful One, who hast created all things, who knowest all things and can do all things, from whom nothing is hidden, to whom nothing is impossible; thou who knowest that we perform not these ceremonies to tempt thy power, but that we may penetrate into the knowledge of hidden things; we pray thee by thy Sacred Mercy to cause and to permit, that we may arrive at this understanding of secret things, of whatever nature they may be, by thine aid, O Most Holy ADONAI, whose Kingdom and Power shall have no end unto the Ages of the Ages. Amen."

Prayer for the mirror (modified from the DSIC operation): "Oh, God! Who art the author of all good things, strengthen, I beseech thee, thy poor servant, that he may stand fast, without fear, through this dealing and work; enlighten, I beseech thee, oh Lord! the dark understanding of thy creature, so that his spiritual eye may be opened to see and know any spirits descending here in this glass." (Then, place your hands over dark mirror or orb.) "And thou, oh inanimate creature of God, be sanctified and consecrated and blessed to this purpose, that no evil phantasy may appear in thee; or, if they do gain ingress into this creature, they may be constrained to speak intelligibly, and truly, and without the least ambiguity, for Christ's sake. Amen. And forasmuch as thy servant here standing before thee, oh, Lord! desires neither evil treasures, nor injury to his neighbor, nor hurt to any living creature, grant him the power of descrying those celestial spirits or intelligences, that may appear in this crystal, and whatever good gifts whether the power of healing infirmities, or of imbibing wisdom, or discovering any evil likely to afflict any person or family, or any other good gift thou mayest be pleased to bestow on me, enable me, by thy wisdom and mercy, to use whatever I may receive to the honor of thy holy name. Grant this for thy son Christ's sake. Amen."

At this time, you should light any charcoals if you are using incense and allow them to become red hot before placing small amounts of incense mixture upon them. Once you are ready, close your eyes and begin to quiet your thoughts; feel every part of your body relaxing and being relieved of all tension. Become aware of your circle of protection and connection to the divine, and know you are safe and in control of all that happens within it. Breathe easily and naturally.

After centering yourself in this way and speaking the aforementioned prayers aloud, light the candles on either side of your scrying device and position them so that neither of the flames can be seen reflected on the surface. Sometimes, it helps to place them a bit further behind your mirror or sphere so that they do not reflect or distract.

Essentially, you want to scry without consciously trying to contact or imagine anything for as long as you can without daydreaming or wondering off in your own mind. Full attention should be given to the mirror as if you were staring out a window during a dark night, expecting to see something. Continue to gaze into the mirror or crystal while remaining perfectly relaxed and do not hesitate to blink when necessary. There is no reason to stress or strain your eyes in any way. Soften the focus of your gaze, but remain attentive and receptive. After a while, the surface of the mirror will begin to change and fade and a dark mist will appear.

In the beginning, "wisps" of lights will appear, along with pale bands that seem to slide across the surface. Possibly after several sessions, images and forms will begin to appear, although ill-defined and vague. Colored lights and clearer forms will appear next. Exactly when this will occur and how long between these stages before the next phenomena occurs is entirely based on your own development.

The point, again, is not to attempt to see or contact anything yet. Sometimes, spirits or visions come into focus, as if curious or aware that you see them. Weird images will fade in and out. Do not be startled or excited by this; stay centered in a receptive and open state of mind. The idea is just to 'be" in the present state of scrying without conscious direction. Sometimes, eerie or odd things will appear, but the idea is to observe it without judgment or breaking your focus. This exercise is similar to some forms of meditation where you passively observe the spirit world without any images disturbing your central place of being. This can be a challenging exercise for the new, eager magician who wants to make active contact with the first hint of something appearing. However, I urge the neophyte or beginning scryer to maintain their patience and passive composure to let things develop on their own accord.

Eventually, you will perceive something that doesn't even seem to come from the mirror at all, but from a "no-place" between you and the mirror or stone. Remember to not be distracted by what you see, but allow the images to come and try to remember what you see. Sometimes when this happens, you will become startled and lose focus of what you were looking at. If this occurs, just reset yourself and continue your gazing.

When you have completed your scrying session, consciously begin to return to your ordinary senses. Breathe fully and deeply and remain still until you feel you have completely returned to a normal state of mind. Now, close your eyes and remember all you saw and felt during the scrying or journey. Review your entire experience mentally. Offer a closing prayer if you wish from a suitable grimoire or from our chosen grimoire of DSIC. I recommend covering your dark mirror or sphere in the black silk cloth or linen as soon as you are done. Clear your working space further by opening up the windows and doors to let in air and light. Before departing the working space, make sure the area feels settled and, again, feel free to sprinkle holy water or burn incense. Immediately after, write every detail in a journal used just for this exercise.

It does not particularly matter what you experience, see, or don't see, as long as you continue to practice often, and keep an open mind. As soon as you complete each scrying session again, remember to record the time, astrological occurrences, and moon phase. Even if a session seems relatively uneventful, you'll start to see patterns with a review of your notes. You'll also begin to notice how much you are becoming attuned with various lunar and astrological correspondences and to which ones you are drawn toward. This building of personal magical data will be invaluable to your progress and will help you gain a clearer perspective on how your practice of magic is developing.

The next section covers every piece of magical furniture or equipment that is written about in the Trithemius experiment of Drawing Spirits into

Crystals. I offer my own measurements and dimensions for the items I created, should the reader wish to emulate my designs. Keep in mind that the text does not specify any measurements, save those for the crystal ball. Trial and error, deductive reasoning, and a dash of inspiration led me to create the implements in the manner I have. I encourage anyone desiring to recreate these experiments to read each section with careful consideration, but not blind adherence. As mentioned previously in the text, I include implements of my own design and items which ultimately complemented the ceremony. I give clear indication to which items belong to the historical text and those which I've personally included into the ceremony. As stated before, I leave it to the reader to decide which they would care to incorporate or discard.

The creation aspect of the magical vestments and instruments are, thankfully, coming under more serious consideration than they have in the past. All too often, westerners are eager to get to the conjuration without taking the time and effort it requires to thoroughly understand and recreate a grimoric experiment. Classical magic is a holistic endeavor which requires the fulfillment of each requirement to fully appreciate the magnitude of the art. In the creation aspect of magical equipment, you are establishing the sorts of energetic links that are going to be present with you during the ceremony. The importance of making as many of the implements as possible and treating each with profound respect cannot be over stated. If you wish your ceremonies to yield the type of results the grimoires speak of, this is an area which should not be rushed. To further elaborate this point, read carefully bellow the section given in Agrippa's *Fourth Book of Occult Philosophy*:

And now we come to treat of the Consecrations which, men ought to make upon all instruments and things necessary to be used in this Art: and the vertue of this Consecration most chiefly consists in two things; to wit, in the power of the person consecrating, and by the virtue of the prayer by which the Consecration is made. For in the person consecrating, there is required holiness of Life, and power of sanctifying: both which are acquired by Dignification and Initiation. And that the person himself should with a firm and undoubted faith believe the virtue, power, and efficacie hereof. And then in the Prayer itself by which this Consecration is made, there is required the like holiness; which either solely consisteth in the prayer itself, as, if it be by divine inspiration ordained to this purpose, such as we have in many places of the holy Bible; or that it be hereunto instituted through the power of the Holy Spirit, in the ordination of the Church. Otherwise, there is in the Prayer a Sanctimony, which is not only by itself, but by the commemoration of holy things; as, the commemoration of holy Scriptures, Histories, Works, Miracles, Effects, Graces, Promises, Sacraments and Sacramental things, and the like. Which things, by a certain similitude, do seem properly or improperly to appertain to the thing consecrated.

If you would prefer to perform separate consecrations for each of the magical implements, I would highly recommend using the prayers listed in either *Veritable Key of Solomon* or ones found in the *Books of Occult Philosophy*. The Operation of DSIC begins with the attitude of the magician toward each endeavor of preparation for the ceremony. From the making of the magical equipment to their consecration and treatment thereof and from the maintenance of the body, mind, and soul of the magician, each is an equally important aspect of bringing about the fullest results of the ceremony.

CHAPTER V

THE EQUIPMENT AND
THE PREPARATIONS

he magical implements of DSIC are only as useful as the magician considers them to be since they are an extension of his will in reaching to the divine. The degree of care and attention given to each as divinely consecrated implements will determine the level of their effectiveness in your magical operation. In such, the degree of integrity, intention, and skill that they embody will reflect the strength and tenacity of the crafter. Likewise, the methods and skill you use in their creation will support the overall comprehension and apprehension of the art as a whole.

No doubt gathering all the necessary materials and tools used for the DSIC operation will be a considerable investment for most practitioners. Many of the items are rare or difficult to come by, but I caution against resorting to substitutions or cutting corners. Do not assume that creating the required items will be done in any small amount of time. No parts of a magical ritual should be hurried and the creation of magical implements is important for the overall integration of the ceremony.

THE CRYSTAL SPHERE

According to DSIC, as related in *The Magus,* the first item to obtain is a crystal ball. The text states that the scrying sphere should be about the size of a *"small orange, i.e. about one inch and a half in diameter; which is to be perfectly clear without blemishes."* This is the direct medium that the magus or scryer communicates to the celestial spirits through.

Choosing your crystal "shew stone" or gazing sphere should require careful research and consideration. This will be the direct aperture for beholding the spiritual entities (i.e., Archangels) that you will be contacting. Since this crystal is the symbolic doorway through which these beings will be communicating with you, it should be treated with the utmost respect and discernment in its selection. The first thing prospective workers of the DSIC operations should be made aware of concerning the selection of their crystal ball is the various types that are available for purchase.

The differences in crystal spheres are not always apparent. Be careful when shopping at New Age or rock supply stores as the sellers will not always be knowledgeable or honest about the products they are trying to sell you. The first thing to consider when buying a crystal ball is whether you want a natural quartz crystal or artificial, reconstituted quartz crystal. At first, this question was a no-brainer for me, as I almost always go for the most natural material I can find. If the crystal is perfectly clear with absolutely zero blemishes, it was most likely lab-created. Fused quartz is a man-made material manufactured principally from sands. It is non-crystalline and can be made in a high purity state. The chemical name of fused quartz is *silicon dioxide* or silica.

These crystals are fairly inexpensive and easier to come by. Natural ones are a great way to go if you can afford it and find one the correct size and clarity. They will at least have some imperfections and never be 100% clear...lab-created ones can be 100%.

The crystal ball I experimented with initially was made of reconstituted quartz, and thus, it is completely clear and without blemish, but, of course, artificially made. The best natural ones you can find are quite expensive and never 100% perfect, but are all natural. The clarity of some of the best naturally formed crystal spheres is about 95% clear.

In my own practice, I have not noticed a large difference between the uses of the two different types of spheres. I consecrated each to the purpose of the work and both have worked tremendously, which should be of some conciliation to the wary magician. The only difference was the natural crystal seemed to reflect less the room and physical environment during the times of the initial conjurations. It also had a unique "feel" when consecrating and working with it. However, as I mentioned, both can and do work for this experiment.

If you opt to find a natural quartz crystal sphere, you should hunt around to find the one with the least amount of blemishes or cloudiness as possible. There are near perfect crystal balls out there; you just have to find them and be willing to pay the higher cost if that is your desire. However, like I mentioned, even the lab-created ones work perfectly fine and will not fail you in your experiments.

I purchased two quartz crystal spheres, approximately the recommended size, fairly inexpensively from eBay. You can find many such items at reasonable prices if you search around, although you must be sure of their quality. Having two crystal spheres of the same size worked out very well. I was able to use one for measuring and making sure it fit correctly into the "gold plate," (which is explained later), and didn't worry about scratching the surface during the construction phase.

Before I made my purchase, I debated about the size of the crystal ball I wanted. At first, an inch and a half or 30mm ball seemed rather small. After drawing out some initial concept sketches, it became clear that if the crystal was too large or heavy, it would protrude from the center of the "gold plate" too far and may be difficult to keep in place. After debating the matter, it seemed as if the size of the sphere was not as important as the closeness of the scrying apparatus and the table of practice itself. One needs to be able to gaze directly at the center of the sphere without any peripheral distractions. In actuality, the suggested size of the crystal ball by the text made perfect sense.

As was explained in depth in the previous chapter, scrying with the crystal sphere typically takes a bit of practice. Although some have notably received visions during initial trials (signs of a gifted scryer), most magicians have to work at it to develop their sight. Even with practice, many still find it difficult to receive a suitable vision. Thus, such a situation warrants the invaluable assistance of a scryer-partner. Such was the case with the famous pair Dr. John Dee and Edward Kelly. Dr. Dee, magus and informant to Queen Elizabeth, along with Edward Kelly, recorded the angelic Enochian system of magick as dictated by the angels. Edward Kelly acted as the scryer in this case and transmitted all the information he viewed and heard from the angels to Dee. In this example, Mr. Kelly was much like a translator between two foreign parties. Dee and Kelly's scrying implements are still on display in a museum in the United Kingdom. A great specimen of a crystal sphere *about the size of a small orange, or about one inch and a half in diameter,* is seen sitting not far from a black obsidian scrying mirror.

THE GOLD DISK

After obtaining the main foci for your spirit communication, Trithemius says, "Get a small plate of pure gold to encompass the crystal round one half."

During my initial experimentation, I toyed with variations of what this "gold plate" could look like. Although the depiction of the scrying apparatus is clear in the diagram, it's possible that the written description implied something different. I eventually opted for following the example given on page 128 of *The Magus,* but I wanted to leave the reader with more possibilities to consider.

A piece of gold could be cut into a plate roughly .75" (or .50") x 3". It could then be inscribed with the proper words and symbols, then hammered/bent into a crescent shape or a full circle band (or ring) to support the crystal sphere. The ebony pedestal can have a simple round base to support the gold-wrapped crystal. In this example, YHVH, the Hexagram, Pentagram and cross shape would appear on the inside where the crystal is. The outside of the gold band would depict the four holy Archangel names. This version would feature the names "inside and outside," not "forward and behind." The only instruction that doesn't seem to fit in this is the mention of an *"engraved circle (A) round the crystal with these characters around inside the circle next the crystal."*

The engraving seems somewhat out of place in this example, as it would bisect the gold plate on the inside, near the crystal. It would force the symbols and letters to be drawn on one side or the other. Perhaps what is intended is to have the symbols on one side and YHVH on the other.

Dr. John Dee also utilized a similar crystal gazing device with a gold band wrapping the stone with a gold cross on the top. If the design that I explain below seems too difficult, you may opt to try something like the above example. I cannot say how well it will work because I have not experimented with the above example.

Since I could not afford pure gold for my chosen design, I settled for a plate of new brass. A plate of silver might also be appropriate if the reader has the means to come by one. I first cut the brass plate into a 3.5" circle and then cut a smaller 1.5" hole using a hole-cutter on my drill. After some sanding and correcting, I got the proper shape where the crystal fit snugly in place about half way through.

Before fixing the crystal in place, I used a Dremel tool to engrave the names and symbols which will be discussed below. A powerful way to inscribe each angel's name is to do it on its ruling day and hour during an astrologically agreeable time. I then covered the entire disk in 24k gold leafing. This took me a couple of tries to apply correctly. I had to paint the disk a metallic gold color before I could get the gold leafing to adhere properly. The end result turned out beautifully and I used black paint to go over the Names and symbols I previously engraved. The directions given in DSIC say:

Engrave a circle around the crystal with these characters:

*Also include them around the inside of the circle next the crystal. Then, afterwards, the name '**Tetragrammaton**'. On the other side of the gold disk is to be engraved the Archangel names: **Michael, Gabriel, Uriel, Raphael.***

The text goes on to state that these angels are *the four principal angels ruling over the Sun, Moon, Venus* and *Mercury*. However, I have come to believe this as a textual error since Archangel Uriel is not attributed to the planet Venus in any other occult texts that I am aware of. Likewise, it seems improbable that Uriel was meant to be replaced with Anael as the fourth angel. Barrett or a scribe may have copied a magical text down incorrectly or may have incidentally attributed Uriel to Venus.

Another textual discrepancy is that the order of the Angelic names reads differently than what is shown on the diagram drawing of the pedestal. On the diagram, Raphael's and Uriel's positions are switched, but I prefer it as it is written above since I'm used to these angels being in that order. The four angels, Raphael, Michael, Gabriel, and Uriel, create a network of control within their oppositional positions to one another. Archangel Anael just did not seem to fit in that equation in my assessment.

My personal conclusion was that Archangel Uriel, "The Fire of God," was not to be omitted and stands as a quarter watcher to grave workings of the universe, a prime mover "of the four." Thus, the Sun, Moon, Mercury, and Uranus are the prime forces of balance and order. Uranus may be substituted as the counter and complementary hidden sphere to Saturn. So in the above example, the light and dark polarities are represented by the Sun and Moon, and movement and exchange versus stability and reservation are embodied by Mercury and Uranus. The names of the Archangels are engraved on the reverse side of the gold disk.

Meditate on the balancing forces of each Archangel. It begins to make better sense when all of the correspondences are looked at. Plus, Archangel Uriel is involved in magical Intentions of the "unexpected and the force of magnetism, all inspiration, astrology and matters of commitment severity," just as we have the "four kings of the four corners of the earth" inscribed on our ritual "foundation" of the Holy Table. The four balancing Archangels are written around in the gold disk as equally balancing and governing celestial powers.

THE EBONY PEDESTAL

The next phase of construction is to mount the gold disk with the crystal ball on "an ivory or ebony pedestal." As I did with the gold disk, I drew a few versions of what this pedestal could look like, but I eventually ended up going for what appears in the diagram shown in *The Magus*.

A fascinating parallel to what the pedestal may have also/actually looked like is what is pictured (MS 48) in the rare manuscript called *Occult Spells, A Nineteenth Century Grimoire*, a work I mentioned earlier in the "History" section, compiled by Frederick Hockley. On pages 29 and 30 in the addition edited and introduced by Silens Manus (The Teitan Press, 2009), the work records accounts of a device utilizing a beryl stone that the text describes as a *"kind of crystal that hath a weak tincture of red"* (MS page 45). Most likely what it is referring to is a type of red, emerald crystal. It shows a round stone encompassed by a gold disk almost identical to the diagram shown in *The Magus*.

Reference to using a scryer or an assistant, such as the one found in the operation of *Abramelin the Mage*, is made when it later states, *"The Magicians now use a crystal sphere or mineral pearl for the purpose which is inspected by a boy or sometimes by the querent himself. They use certain Formulas of prayer to be used before they make the inspection which they term a call"* (MS 46).

MS page 47 reveals the image of the consecrated beryl stone, according to the author of *Occult Spells*. On this page is the depiction, which is strikingly similar to the gold disk found in *The Magus*. It has a large ring encompassing the stone. The ring has "MICHAEL-GABRIEL-URIEL-RAPHAEL" written around it. Instead of the "house" type pedestal, which *The Magus* shows, an intricate pillar supports the disk and stone. The description near the illustration reads:

> *This Beryll is a Perfect Sphere, the diameter I guess to be of something more than an inch, it is set in a ring or circle of silver resembling the Meridian of a Globe, the stem of it is about 10 inches high all gilt at the 4 quarters of it and the names of 4 angels viz, Uriel, Gabriel, Michael, Raphael on the top is a cross patee (MS page 48).*

The illustration also shows an equilateral cross located at the top. You may recall that one of Dr. Dee's crystal *shew* stones had a cross located at the top — one more example that demonstrates how each of these works had a common source.

For my ebony pedestal, I bought a board of black Gaboon ebony wood which was quite expensive. Ebony stems from a Greek word that means "fruit of the gods" and they believed that drinking from goblets made from this wood would be an antidote for poisons. It was also used in magic to thwart an enemy's evil intent. Species of the ebony tree number in the hundreds worldwide, but most are only shrubs, and only one type is found to grow in North America. The ebony tree most commonly used for lumber are found on the Asian, Indian, and African continents.

Ebony trees can grow to fifty feet in height and one and a half feet in diameter. Most trees are over a hundred years old and, thus, supplies of all sorts of ebony are in relatively limited supply. The wood ended up costing me about eighty dollars for a 4"x 4' plank. I decided to cut the board to the similitude of the diagram shown in the book.

From the dimensions given on the size of the crystal, I figured a 4"x4" main square would contain the gold disk and crystal in the center nicely while another 2" could be left for the top where the star and spire are located. I made the bottom post 1.5"x1.5" and the base 2"x2". The circle in the center was cut with a 3.5" circle cutter on a drill. The tools needed to do this were also costly, but worth it, as ebony wood is *very* hard/dense and difficult to cut by hand.

The base and small post is not shown in the diagram in *The Magus* but used in other versions I have seen. I used small amounts of wood glue to keep the ebony wood pieces together and a strong clear epoxy resin to keep the gold disk and crystal sphere firmly in place. If you are unable to buy any of the needed tools to cut your board, I would recommend finding a wood worker who could personally assist you with cutting your ebony wood precisely. The materials are simply too valuable and costly to make mistakes with.

Ebony pedestal front side   Ebony pedestal back side

THE HOLY TABLE

The Magus mentions that once the ebony pedestal with the crystal in the gold disc is created, it should sit on a table with various other names, seals, and symbols, as well as the four kings:

> *On the table on which the crystal stands the following names, characters, &c. must be drawn in order. First, the names of the seven*

planets and angels ruling them, with their seals or characters. The names of the four kings of the four corners of the earth. Let them be all written within a double circle, with a triangle on a table; on which place the crystal on its pedestal: this being done, thy table is complete and fit for the calling of the spirits.

The "table" Trithemius is referring to is known as the Holy Table, or Table of Practice/Art. Notice specifically the section where Trithemius states that *"on the table on which the crystal stands the following names, characters, &c.* ***must be drawn in order"*** [emphasis added]. This sentence stuck out to me after years of working with the *Goetia*. The magic circle used in the *Goetia* lists a series of divine names, angels, and planets in a particular descending order which is found in many other grimoric works. This order is based on Heinrich Cornelius Agrippa's "Scale of Ten." It is commonly referred to as the "***Chaldean Order.***" The *Schema huius praemiffae diuifionis Sphaerarum* shows the descending order of planets in a pictorial diagram of widening circles. By studying this diagram and constantly paying attention to planetary hours and their sequences, one can easily determine the proper order the angels should be listed in.

Note in the diagram below (going outside to inside), we are given the order of SATVRNI (Saturn), IOVIS (Jupiter), MARTIS (Mars), SOLIS (Sun), VENERIS (Venus), MERCVRII (Mercury), and LUNAE (Moon).

Thus, the names of the planets and their angels should be written or engraved in the order mentioned above and followed accordingly. The text says to list the names of the seven planets and angels ruling them with their seals or characters. The "seals" are the Archangel's sigils and planetary symbols, which also appear on the lamens and magic circle of the DSIC experiment. The sigils and symbols are same ones depicted in *the DISPOSITIO Numerorum Magica Ab Unitate Usque ad DVODENARIVM Collecta,* or *Magical Calendar.* These famous sigils of the Archangels are used in many, if not most, classical works of western occultism.

The angels along with their sigils and seals should be written around the edge of the Holy Table in an unbroken circle. The next step is to write or engrave the names of the "four kings" within a second circle:

> *The names of the four kings of the four corners of the earth. Let them be all written within a double circle, with a triangle on a table; on which place the crystal on its pedestal: this being done, thy table is complete and fit for the calling of the spirits.*

The identities of the *"four Kings of the cardinal directions"* have been the subject of some debate and much confusion in the occult community. Indeed, few grimoires seem to agree on which names go where and which names are to be used in the first place. In working with *Lemegeton,* I had become accustomed to dealing with the four kings, which are mentioned in the *Goetia.* These are: Amaymon in the East, Corson in the West, Ziminar in the North, and Goap in the South. However, as Joseph Peterson points out on his indispensable *Esoteric Archives* website:

> *Agrippa, OP2.7 has (E, W, N, S): "Oriens.Paymon.Egyn.Amaymon", however, later he states in OP3.24, "Urieus, King of the East; Amaymon, King of the South; Paymon, King of the West; Egin, King of the North, which the Hebrew Doctors perhaps call more rightly thus, Samuel, Azazel, Azael, Mahazuel…*

> *Another source from the Cichus In Sphaeram Mundi, f. 21 apud quem: Zoroa. Fragm. O104; cf. Salom. ff. 28v-29r; sed addict. K: Reuchl. Arte 3, sig. O7r) MC has: "Bael, Moymon, Poymon, Egyn" or "Asmodel in the East, Amaymon in the South, Paymon in the West, and Aegym*

in the North"; "Oriens, Paymon, Egyn, and Amaymon"; or "Amodeo [sic] (king of the East), Paymon (king of the West), Egion (king of the North), and Maimon.

After some research into the names and working between the various manuscripts which mention them, I settled on four names that seem to be used the most often from older texts. The four names I use on my Table of Practice are in the following directions: Oriens in the East, Amaymon in the South, Paymon in the West, and Egyn in the North.

ORIENS + AMAYMON + PAYMON + EGYN

The "Four Kings" of *Lemegeton* act as the wardens (and, in some cases, also one of the possible spirits to evoke) for all the other spirits. Each of these four has a collection of spirits which are under their control and direction. These four are who you petition to cause any spirit to appear if they do not arrive after your initial invocations. I have never attempted to directly invoke one of these "demon kings of the directions," but consider them very potent beings. *Lemegeton* warns that "they are not to be called forth except it be upon great occasions but Invoked & commanded to send such & such spirit as [is] under their rule and power, as is shewed in ye following Invocations, or [rather] conjurations &c."

I found it interesting that DSIC mentions "the four kings of the four corners of the earth," and, although no names are actually given for these kings, it quite clear to what the author is referring. It is not a repeat of the four Archangels who are to be inscribed on the gold disk. The four kings are the ones mentioned in a number of grimoires who have dominion over the four directions of the world. Certainly these rulers are spirits of significant power and authority. Some scholars and practicing magicians have difficulty adding them in with their angelic workings as their names are quite popular among the Arch demons in the previously mentioned grimoires. They are acknowledged by various names and titles (usually kings or princes) and can be considered as being the gatekeepers of the physical plane who allow spirits to have interaction with the world in a very controlled manner. In this role, they are less concerned with direct involvement in human affairs and more so in the control of traffic and interaction with the world of matter.

Although I have yet to conjure and ask one of the demon princes or kings directly or question one of the angels directly about them, I've conceived them to be powerful beings with specific offices of moderation and control. That is to say that their primary assignment (office) is the oversight and border control of every spirit's exchange and influence allotted on the physical plane/earth, as well as with whom or what. They seem to strictly enforce the time, direction, office, and level of interaction permitted between the worlds. In the fulfillment of these duties as dictated by a/the higher, they are effectively "masters" of the world in their own direction and area. Just like no one element rules supreme over the others in the laws of balance in creation, so too do these spirits split the control between themselves. Perhaps by design and association, from the lowest earthbound spirit to the near highest celestial choir, the four kings arrange and moderate each "visitor" who interacts with creation. At any rate, they are specifically included as part of this art of conjuration as they are in many classical works. They have their own "ring" on the Holy Table and act as wardens to each of the four directions. Their aspects and roles in conjuration should be understood and integrated into the magician's workings.

The table of practice I use was made from a ten-inch disk of wood. I used masking tape to cover the whole face and drew out two circles. One was an eight-inch outer ring and a seven-inch inner ring. The triangle was approximately six inches on each side. I wood-burned the designs and then engraved the four cardinal kings in Greek lettering, plus four cross quarter crosses. This is how they appear:

ΟΡΙΕΝΣ + ΑΜΑΥΜΟΝ + ΠΑΥΜΟΝ + ΕΓUN

The triangle and rings were painted white and the spaces between painted in black. The boarder on the rings and triangle received gold leafing to add a wonderful effect.

I enjoy the old spelling of the planets in the *Schema huius praemiffae diuifionis Sphaerarum*: SATVRNI (Saturn), IOVIS (Jupiter), MARTIS (Mars), SOLIS (Sun), VENERIS (Venus), MERCVRII (Mercury), and LUNAE (Moon), so I decided to use this on my Holy Table. Each of the seven sections was also painted in the corresponding color of the planets. I debated for a time whether I wanted to use English, Hebrew, or angelic script for the names of the angels and planets. I believe any of these choices are valid and would be appropriate. However, I eventually settled on the English versions, since this is the language I will be requiring the angels to speak to me in.

As to the material considerations used to make the Holy Table, I personally made mine out of a disk of oak wood, but realized other materials could possibly be used instead. White beeswax (similar to what Dr. John Dee used to construct his *Sgillum Dei Ameth*) might be an appropriate choice. Again, the text gives no mention or instruction as to what the Holy Table is to be made out of so we are able to speculate. Purified beeswax is recommended to be used for making many magical seals and talismans. Another idea would be to make the Holy Table from a precious metal, such as gold or silver. I designed a few concepts of what the Holy Table could consist of and found that wax, wood, metal, or a combination could work.

The Holy Table

Holy Table with Ebony Pedestal

Two candles are set on either side of the *Holy Table* or Table of Practice. The side note next to the diagram in *The Magus* says that the candle sticks are to be made of silver. I use two silver-plated candle sticks and two bees-wax candle tappers, which are lit at the beginning of the ceremony. Another idea to consider is to use colored candles, which correspond to the planetary intelligence you are working with, i.e., black for Saturn, blue for Jupiter, red for Mars, yellow for the Sun, green for Venus, orange or multicolored for Mercury, and silver for the Moon. The candles should be new and unused for every evocation. Although it is not necessary to do so, I have experimented with lacing the candles with a drop of appropriate planetary or angelic fluid condenser. The added corresponding effects when the tapers are lit seem to add that much more conducive atmosphere for the evocation.

Holy Table, Ebony pedestal, and Silver Candlesticks

The Wand

The ebony wand, with its gold-gilt holy names, is truly a powerful instrument and the only item that is held in the hand during the ceremony. Unless you decide to also hold the incense tripod, your wand will be handled for the majority of the operation. The first mention of the ebony wand in DSIC is after the opening prayer at the beginning of the operation. It says to: *Take your black ebony wand, with the gilt characters on it and trace the circle.* This will be its first, but not only function during the course of the operation. Through use and experience, you will come to realize the powerful nature of this classical instrument of magic.

The ebony wand will be your primary symbol of divine authority; great care should be taken in its construction and use. The ebony wood you use for its construction should be as near perfect as possible without any cracks or blemishes along its surface. Handling the raw material before and during construction should be done with reverent attention. *The Magus* is unique in its suggestion to use ebony wood for the material of the magic wand.

Joseph Peterson, on his site, www.esotericarchives.com, describes ebony as having the following qualities: *"Ebony is named as the wood of Hermes in one ancient Greek spell (Faraone, p. 202.) The Egyptian king, Nectanebus, used a rod or wand of ebony, along with magic formulae to animate models of his enemies and attack them. (Budge, 1930, p. 488; 1971, p. 92.) An Ebony wand is used in the Graeco-Egyptian spell PGM I.335 (Betz p. 12).*

Due to the particular Mercurial symbol of wands and compounding nature of ebony, it seems appropriate to construct it on the day and hour of Mercury (Wednesday on the first hour of the day). Luckily, the dimensions of my ebony plank were enough to construct all the needed implements which required it. My wand was made from the same stock as my ebony pedestal with some left over. The finest section of the ebony wood plank was first cut to a 1x1-inch square post. Then, it was wood-turned into a dowel rod by a master wood carver I met while learning how to hone my own wood-working skills.

During the phase of a waxing moon, I awoke twenty minutes before the first hour of Mercury on a Wednesday morning. I washed, recited a Solomonic consecration prayer, and anointed my hands and temples with holy oil. As the hour came upon me, I presented my soon-to-be wand to the eastern sky and drew as much divine energy into me as I could muster. While practicing some energetic breathing, I began sanding the ebony rod until it was smooth, each breath raising my energy with the repetitive action. When I felt it was finished and filled with the combined energy of the time and my efforts, I cut to the desired size and took it within the house. I engraved the holy names with a Solomonic style burin, and gold leafed with the following names and characters:

(on the reverse side was engraved the below)

εγω το Αλφα και το ω

I decided to use the phrase and alphabet used in the Greek language for "I am the Alpha and Omega," as it seemed to be appropriate and stayed within the original context. The end result turned out quite well, as you can see below.

Ebony Wand Side A

Εγο το Αλφα και το Ω

Ebony Wand Side B

There is a wand of very similar design depicted in *A Complete Book of Magic Science*. However, the names show "Alpha" and "Omega" on opposite ends of the wand with "Tetragrammaton Saday" in the center. The manuscript does not say what the wand is to be made of.

Gold leafing or gilding takes some practice to do well, but is by no means difficult. I used the smallest paint brush I could find to apply the gilding glue to the engraved characters and waited for it to become clear and tacky. I then lightly applied the gold leaf and let it set for a few minutes before brushing over it with a soft paint brush. Eventually, the unfixed flakes fell away, leaving beautiful gold letters.

Often, the exact size and shape of the wand is missing or unclear in the grimoires with only minimal references to diagrams picturing possible dimensions. After referring to and comparing several well-known grimoires, I've come to appreciate the wide array and variation of this popularized magical instrument. I do not think the wand used for our operation needs to be any exact size or shape. My ebony wand for DSIC is approximately eighteen inches long, which matches the measurement from the tip of my index conger to my elbow. This method is popular among magicians and one I use to personalize my wands. Various lengths are mentioned throughout the Solomonic texts, such as *Veritable Key of Solomon*, which seem to allude to a wide range of personal preference.

Aggripa's *Fourth Book* and *The Magus* both do not have any instructions that I recall for the constructing of the magic wand. Lengths between seventeen to twenty inches seem to encompass most measurements for the wand/verga.

The thickness of my wand is near to the width of my index finger, at about .75". I've read where some wands are supposed to be up to an inch thick. As with a few other items where the text is not strictly descriptive of the measurements of ritual implements, I opted for informed intuition and comparison to similar grimoires. After constructing a number of wands through my magical career and having ample experience with each, I am a firm believer that the wand should "feel" correctly in your hands. Without straying into "New Age" generalities, I believe this intuitive concept is important, as the wand should naturally feel as an extension of your will, even before consecration of it. It should be crafted by you, with all the detail and gold gilding definitely done by your own hand. The work and effort you put into all the tools will be a mixture of your own ingenuity and energy, combined with their intended purpose and use in ritual. I recommend not only crafting your wand during a beneficial hour of Mercury but consecrating it then, as well. Crafting, obtaining, and consecrating most of your tools on this day and hour is a good idea in fact. The times and days where it would differ is when you are crafting names, seals, or sigils pertaining to a certain planetary spirit, angel, or intelligence. For instance, I chose to craft my Michael/Sun talisman on the first beneficial Sun hour on Sunday. I would try to use this method for magical timing for creating every piece of magical equipment you plan on using in the ritual. With western ceremonial magic, the more positive correspondences you can put into a thing, the better.

The material (ebony) and magical formula used for this wand is quite magnificent with potent meaning in its composition. If ebony wood indeed has characteristics and attributes corresponding to the energies of Mercury, it is perfectly suited toward working with spirits. It is known that the name of God, "AGLA," was used by Jewish Kabbalists as the powerful invocation for exorcizing and controlling a plethora of spirits. AGLA is comprised of the four Hebrew letters: "Athah Gobon Leolam Adonai" or "Thou art the powerful and eternal Lord." "ON" is somewhat mysterious, but has been translated as meaning "pillar" or "support" in a Hebrew context, likened to the word "Sumelch." In translation, the words on the wand could literally mean:

"By the most Powerful and Eternal Lord, I am supported by Him who Is, and eternally Is," or "Oh most powerful and eternal Lord, support me, my God, who is and eternally is."

The wand is meant to be a representation of divine authority and command. As such, it should be treated with the upmost respect and dignity at all times. This is not and was never meant to only be a "director of the magician's will." This is also not a "blasting rod" in which to threaten or subdue spirits with either. It is wielded as an active symbol of holy diplomacy and ambassadorship. When you invoke holy Archangels with this wand, you are doing so with the assumption of divine inspiration and permission.

The wand is also used in tracing out the protective circle during the initial phase of the ceremony as was explained previously. Whatever it touches or is directed at is the embodiment of the Most Holy. Afterward, it is to be held vertically in the right (predominant) hand while invoking the spirit and then changed to the left hand when bidding the spirit farewell.

As you may have noticed, I did not use the popular phrase, "*banish the spirit.*" This is intentional, due to the nature of the initial spirits which this system is intended to bring forth. These are celestial planetary intelligences and not demons or earthbound spirits. I plan on dealing with those types of beings in another work. The divine nature of the Archangels allot them a certain measure of respectful diplomacy. Magicians have varying opinions about how an angel is to be treated, but I assure you that you want to go with respectful composure any time you are dealing with an ascended intelligence. Far more knowledge and assistance will be garnered if these beings are treated as one would a highly respected master or teacher.

It is not exactly clear which Hebrew letter is depicted within the hexagram on the wand. The diagrams in *The Magus* seem to show a hexagram star with a mark in the center on not only the wand, but possibly the gold disk and ebony pedestal, as well. At first, I thought it was a simple Yod, but further consideration led me to believe it was in fact a Dalet. This Hebrew character can have the singular reference to represent the Names of God and thus, make sense to be carved on the same side as the Tetragrammaton. It has been used in reference to the sacred names without actually spelling out the word and also in reference to the crown or Kether on the Tree of Life. It seems most appropriate to use this particular Hebrew character on not only your wand, but the ebony pedestal, as well.

THE ROBE

A particular ceremonial robe such as one made from virgin linen or silk is not listed as one of the requisites in DSIC. However, ritual attire, or *priestly* garments, should be assumed due to the genre of grimoric traditions and nature of the invocations. White linen or silk are the traditional fabrics used in practically every grimoire. These robes, or more appropriately, albs, are the common ritual attire of the Catholic priesthood.

If we refer to *A Complete Book of Magic Science,* we see the magical attire consists of vestments and a girdle. There is no description of either beyond them "being pure," but a blessing is given for each. I've included the prayer below in the instance where the reader wishes to include it in their operation. The text of DSIC gives no benedictions or consecrations for the robe or ring, but does so for the circle, crystal, and perfumes/fire.

Benediction of the Garment:

O Holy, blessed and Enternal Lord God Who art the God of purity and delightest that our souls should appear before Thee in clean and pure and undefiled Vestments grant o Lord that these Garments being cleansed, blessed, and consecrated by Thee, I may put them on, and being therewith clothed I may be whiter than snow both in soul and body in Thy presence this day, in and through the Merits, death, and passion of our only Lord and Savior Jesus Christ, Who liveth and reigneth with Thee in the Unity of the Holy Spirit, ever one God, world without end. The God of Abraham, The God of Isaac, the God of Jacob bless thee, purge thee, and make pure, and be thou clean in the Name of the Father, Son, and Holy Ghost, Amen, (make sign of the cross) Per hoc Crucis Signum fugiat procul omne Malignum et per idem Signum Salvetur quodque benignum (make sign of cross).

A girdle is also mentioned as part of the magical vestments. A typical cincture, a belt cord would be the usual choice to wrap around your priestly garment. The colors corresponding to the planetary intelligence you are contacting would be well-suited. Little is said of girdles or belts in magical grimoires, save for the lion skin belt of the *Goetia*. Such an item might be appropriate, due to the planetary names, angels, and names of God associated with each sphere being written on the belt. If you decide to utilize a "magician's girdle," it does not have to be made from animal skin like the lion belt mentioned above, but should be fashioned from natural fabric, such as cotton, linen, or silk.

A blessing for the girdle is given in *A Complete Book of Magic Science:*

O God, Who by the breath of Thy nostrils framed heaven and Earth and wonderfully disposed of all things therein in six days, grant that this now brought to perfection by Thine unworthy servant may be my Thee blessed and receive Divine virtue, power, and Influence from Thee that everything therein contained may fully operate according to the hope and confidence of me, Thine unworthy servant through Jesus Christ our Lord Savior. Amen

(Then Sprinkle it with Holy water: Asperges me domine hysopo et mundabo Lavabis et Supra Nivi Dealbabor miserere me dues secudum Magnam Misericordiam tuam et Supra nivein dealbor Gloria patri et filio et Spiritu I Sancto sicut erat in principio est nunc et Saecula Saeculorum. Amen).

A fairly modern idea is to wear a colored robe suited to the planetary intelligence you will be working with. Again, these color correspondences are black for Saturn, royal blue or purple for Jupiter, red for Mars, yellow or gold for the Sun, green for Venus, orange or multi-colored for Mercury, and silver for the Moon. If working with a partner or scryer, it is assumed both of you will be dressed similarly to harmonize with the nature of the ceremony.

For an additional article to add to your magical attire, I recommend also wearing a stole. For this magical operation, it would be suitable to wear a colored stole appropriate to the planetary intelligence. This priestly vestment can be adorned or embroidered with planetary symbols and sigils to better connect you with the celestial beings you are trying to summon. I have seen historic illustrations of wizard-conjures wearing a sort of deacon style stole or "award sash" with astrological images written around the entire circumference. These early drawings inspired me to create a set of the planetary stoles I now wear in my rituals. I painted the primary planetary symbol along with the main sigils and character of the planet on seven linen stoles in appropriate colors. The planetary stole is not listed in the DSIC operation, but one I include in my personal practice.

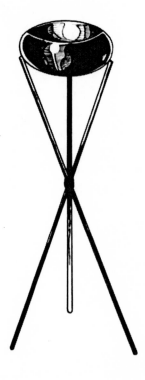

THE TRIPOD

The DSIC operation includes a piece of magical equipment which the text describes as a tripod. *The Magus* describes this as being the instrument where the perfumes of the art are to be placed. An illustration shows what looks like a torch with three brackets at the top and either smoke or flames issuing from it. Two very similar diagrams are depicted along with a wand in *A Complete Book of Magic Science,* no doubt of similar origin.

The note next to the tripod drawing says it may be "either held in the hand or set in the earth," which I took to mean that it is either held while in the circle or set outside of it. The first option seemed rather cumbersome and unnecessary, so I opted for a self-supporting censor.

This type of tripod can be placed upon the ground or embedded as a spike into the earth, which would work best if you were outside. If not held by the magician or scryer, it is to *be placed between the circle and the Holy Table.* For the construction of my tripod, I bought three brass poles which were thirty-six inches in height and a new silver bowl about four inches wide. I also bought brass and red metal wire to be used to hold the silver censor bowl. Everything was supported by the brass legs. I used the metal wire to wrap each pole individually and together about three inches down from the top so that they acted as the supporting legs of the tripod without slipping. I made another circle of brass wire with three feet that went into the holes of the top of the poles. I also wove thin wiring into the circle to form a sort of wire basket that could support the incense burner. The design was fairly simple and efficient, and it took me about ten minutes to make.

The tripod is easily set up and taken down, and it stands at just the right height for my table on which the Holy Table and pedestal rests. I placed thin wire mesh in the silver bowl just about half way down which acts as the seat for the charcoal. Lit charcoals burn effortlessly with the flow of oxygen underneath. Once the incense is placed upon the coals, the rising smoke drifts upward near the pedestal and throughout the working room. Whatever your choice or design for the tripod incense burner, it should be easily accessible during your ritual and within reach to add more incense mixture as you chose. It should also be light enough to move in and out of the circle with ease.

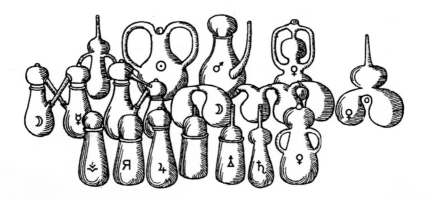

THE PERFUMES OF ART

Every grimoire has a slightly different assortment of applicable and corresponding *suffumigations* or incense blends to be utilized. Each ingredient should have correlation to the type of planetary spirit you are summoning. I've experimented with a wide range of classic incenses and even some of the newer mixtures with varying results. I've decided to include four varieties listed in grimoires I felt were most appropriate for this work, and also those I've had the greatest success with.

Each planetary mixture should be created on the proper day and hour of the associated planet to further imbue the perfume with corresponding energies. Gather your ingredients ahead of time and select those that seem most agreeable and pure.

In practice and procedure, *A Complete Book of Magic Science* (BoM) is the grimoire which corresponds closest to the operation of DSIC. It contains a list of ingredients that are used as planetary suffumigations to evoke forth the planetary or *Olympic Spirits*. This list of associated planetary spirits and perfume mixtures is also found in *The Secret Grimoire of Turiel*. Some of the ingredients differ widely from those found in other magical works and appear to be mixed up between the days and planets. Although included here, I have not experimented widely with these particular concoctions. I prefer those listed in the next three categories and have had very agreeable results.

The next list of perfumes will be those found in the *Heptameron*. Barrett includes the operation of the *Heptameron* before DSIC within *The Magus*. Keep in mind, some of these perfumes are intended more for lower planetary spirits and demons rather than angels. Some might be more agreeable to angels than others. Besides the basic *Heptameron* ingredients, I have listed the ingredients prescribed in *Veritable Key of Solomon*. I found these ingredients to be the most agreeable for the Archangels than the previous two. In the original texts, blood and flesh of certain animals are mentioned which I have omitted. For the full recipe, see *Veritable Key of Solomon* by Stephen Skinner and David Rankine, and *The Complete Book of Magic Science* by Hockley.

Finally, I will include the incenses suggested by Agrippa from his works of *Occult Philosophy*. Out of these selections, the practicing magician should find plenty of ingredients to experiment with. The suggested incense blends are listed below.

The Perfume of the Lord's Day (Sunday)/Michael

BoM:	Black Pepper Grains, Hogsbane Grains, Powder of Loadstone, Myrrh of the East
Heptameron:	Red Wheat* (Red Sandalwood)
VKoS:	"Saffron, Amber, Musk, Aloes Wood, Balm Wood, Laurel seeds, Cloves, Myrrh and Frankincense — these herbs should all be a sixth of an ounce, with the exception of amber and musk, which should only be a grain each."
Agrippa:	"Benzoin, Storax, Oliibanum, Labdanum, Galbanum"

The Perfume of Monday/Gabriel

BoM:	Euphorbe, Baellium, Sal Amomonian, Roots of Helibore, Powder of Loadstone and a little Sulfur
Heptameron:	Aloes (Lignum Aloes)
VKoS:	"A white Poppy seed, the most exquisite Incense and a small amount of Camphor"
Agrippa:	"Myrtle leaf, Clary sage, Davana, Geranium, Wormwood, Eucalyptus, Rosemary"

The Perfume of Tuesday/ Samael

BoM:	White Poppy, Storax, Loadstone, Benjamin, Camphor, Chamomile Flowers
Heptameron:	Pepper or Black ground pepper (Actually, most likely Costus root, Sausurea Lappa)
VKoS:	"Euphorbia, Belladonna, Ammonia Salt, roots from two Hellebores, Powder of magnetized stone and a small amount of Sulfur"
Agrippa:	"Cedar Wood, Red Sandalwood, Cypress, Rosewood"

The Perfume of Wednesday/Raphael

BoM:	The seed of an Ash tree, Aloe Wood, Storax, Blue Loadstone Powder, and the end of a Quill
Heptameron:	Mastic
VKoS:	"Oriental Mastic, any Incense of choice, Cloves, Pentaphylla flowers, powder of Agate"
Agrippa:	"Cinnamon, Coriander, Cardamom, Musk seeds, Anise, Blood orange, Bergamot"

The Perfume of Thursday/ Sachiel

BoM:	Mastic of the East, chosen Incense, Cloves, Powder of Agate
Heptameron:	Saffron
VKoS:	"Rowan Berry, Wood of Aloes, Storax Benzoin, Powder of Lapis Lazuli, pieces of chopped up Peacock feathers" (I've used this concoction many times, minus the animal blood and flesh parts, and it works wonderfully!)
Agrippa:	"Clove, Allspice, Star Anise, Juniper Berries, Vanilla, Peppercorn, Nutmeg"

The Perfume of Friday/Anael

BoM: Musk, Ambergris, Wood of Aloes, Dried Red Roses, Red Coral

Heptameron: Pepperwort (*Costus is probably referring to Saussurea lappa, not pepperwort –note by Joseph H. Peterson*)

VKoS: "Musk, Ambergris, Aloes Wood, Dried Red Roses, Red Coral"

Agrippa: "Safflower Petals, Jasmine Flowers, Larkspur Flowers, Rose Petals, Ylang Ylang"

The Fumigation of Saturday/Cassiel

BoM: Saffron, Aloe Wood, Balsam of Myrrh, add to it a Grain of Musk, and Ambergris

Heptameron: Sulfur (Caution must be used when burning this; the fumes can be noxious!)

VKoS: A Black Poppy Seed, Henbane Seed, Mandrake Root, Powdered Magnet Stone and a good, quality Powdered Myrrh

Agrippa: Frankincense, Costus, Calamus, Bdellium, Spikenard, Galangal, Ginger, Vetiver, Zedoary.

It should be noted that some of these incenses can be toxins or irritants if inhaled in large doses. Tuesday's and Saturdays' incenses are most dangerous. Caution should be taken and proper ventilation assured before conducting any experiment. It may be wise to practice with these components to see how well you fare with them before using them in an actual operation.

THE MAGIC RING

A ring is mentioned as part of the evocation equipment. However, there is neither a description, nor an illustration of the ring given within the text. There is also no mention as to what it is to be made from. All the text states is to, "*take your ring and put the ring on the little finger of your right hand.*" Again, I used intuition and deductive reasoning from other source materials to determine what the author most likely intended.

In *The Magus* (106), there are drawings of some magical figures, a wand and a ring. The wand has the same sacred names and symbols as that of the ebony wand. The ring looks like a simple band with a hexagram inscribed upon a disk at the top. In searching for such a suitable requisite, I came upon a silver ring with just such a hexagram on a red enameled background.

Gold or silver are the two most common metals used for magical rings. Silver is preferred for the magic ring in Weyer's version of the *Goetia*. The Lamen is also recommended to be silver, so this seemed more than appropriate. In addition, I had the same names that *Lemegeton* prescribes engraved on the Ring: *Tetragrammaton* on the inside and *Michael — Anaphexiton* on the outside. The magic ring is worn as a symbol of authority and protection. Stories of magic rings seem abundant in every culture that had them. In grimoric tradition, it is Solomon's magic ring that is being represented. When worn, the wearer assumes full command over spirits both benevolent and hostile. Typically, it is engraved with sacred names of God and a *seal* (usually assumed to be the six-pointed star of Seal of Solomon).

The magical ring is a shield of protection and banner of obedience to all spiritual forces. The ring is a perfect symbol of divine unity and the impenetrable armor of God. To the spirit, there is no transgressing past this unified symbol of divine completeness. It is recommended that the ring you use be brand new and used only for this operation. The ring should be sized to fit upon the little finger of your right hand. If you are not in the position to make a ring yourself, you can look for silver rings online, or on an auction site like eBay. I recommend looking into Jewish or Kabalistic jewelry for a suitable choice.

The Lamen

The grimoire of DSIC says that the magical lamen should be made of either silver or of parchment. Specifically, the text states that the lamen is made from a "square plate of silver." This is interesting to note since the example for the lamen given in the text is that of Michael and Sol, or the sun.

One would assume the most appropriate metal to use for a solar

lamen would be gold. As with the magical ring, it's not uncommon for the metal of choice to be either silver or gold for the creation of magical lamens. The sun and moon metals have a large influence over spirits and are the materials suggested for most magic rings, lamens, seals, and other protective talismans. I would recommend beginning with either a silver or parchment lamen for your first few evocations.

Parchment is a term often used in magical grimoires, but is seldom understood or acknowledged by modern practitioners of the art. Virgin Parchment is not simply "paper" that has not been written on or used for anything before. The grimoires are describing something much more valuable and also much rarer in this day and age. *Key of Solomon* indicates the sort of proper parchment used for various magical images. These seals were often used for evocation. There are detailed instructions for the creation of this parchment in *Key of Solomon (KoS)*, as well as a few other select grimoires. As very few of us have direct experience and opportunity (not to mention a taste) for skinning animals, etc., parchment of this sort can be impractical to create. Nonetheless, virgin parchment of this caliber is possible to obtain for a reasonable fee.

First, let's take a look at the description given in *Lemegeton's Goetia* (as given on Joseph Peterson's Esoteric Archives):

> *This figure is to be made on parchment made of a calfes Skin and worne at the Skirtt of ye white vestment, and covered with a lennen [linen] cloath to ye which is to be shewed to the spirits when they are appeared that they may be compelled to be obedient and take a humane shape &c.*

Calfskin parchment is produced from the membrane or hide of a calf. It is particularly valuable, due to its softness and rough grain. Besides being used for writing, parchment was also used for traditional leather bookbinding. Fine calfskin is what the grimoires are referring to when they describe the material used for vellum and parchment manuscripts. *Vellum* is mentioned as the particular parchment required for the *Book of Spirits*, described in DSIC. I explain more about this book in the next chapter.

I found a great website that creates high quality calfskin parchment. If you are interested in creating a seal using this traditional material, you can find them at http://www.pergamena.net/products/parchment/. On their website, they describe the intricacies of calfskin parchment and its use for writing and bookbinding.

When studying the process of how parchment is made, even without the added complexities as *Key of Solomon* describes, one can see an alchemical transformation. Although this type of parchment was more common during the times these grimoires were recorded, the value placed on "virgin parchment" is obviously apparent. From the young virgin animal, the skin becomes parchment only after a process of intense treatment and refinement. The hide first undergoes a shedding of the unneeded and base material in favor of the purified core or essence. It then becomes treated and stretched to form suitable sheets of writing material. Studying the entire process in depth, one may recognize the occult components of salt, sulfur, and mercury.

Regardless of the type of material you will be using, the time and day of its construction should also be a vital part of its creation process. Consideration should also be given to the phase of the moon and any astrological circumstances to determine how potent your timing will be.

For example, if you were planning to evoke Archangel Michael, you would want to create his Lamen on the Day and Hour of the Sun. This means Sunday, at the very first or eighth hour, when the sun rises over the horizon at your physical location. As I mentioned previously, finding the exact times of the planets is quite easy in this day and age, with resources like http://www.astrology.com.tr/planetary-hours.asp. Calculations should be double-checked with other sources to be sure, but there is no need to get too complex. I found it is nice to burn incense appropriate to the angel, as well as keeping my full concentration on his attributes while making lamens.

In Book II of *The Magus* (94), there is a more detailed description of the lamen's construction, which gives the magician more options to work with and consider.

Now the lamen which is used to invoke any good spirit must be made after the following manner: either in metal conformable (meaning agreeable onto the spirits planetary correspondence) or in new wax mixed with convenient spices and colors; or it may be made with pure white paper with convenient colors, and the outward form of it may be either square, circular, or triangular, or of the like sort, according to the rule of numbers, in which there must be written the divine names, as well general as special. And in the center of the lamen, draw a hexagon or character of six corners, in the middle thereof, write the name and character of the star, or of the spirit, his governor, to whom the good spirit that is to be called is subject. And about this character, let there be places so many characters of five corners or pentacles as the spirits as the spirits we would call together at once. But, if we should call only one, nevertheless, there must be made four pentagons, wherein the name of the spirit or spirits, with their characters, are to be written.

The above paragraph offers yet another substance with which to make the spirit's lamen or basic table. It suggests using new wax, which would likely mean purified beeswax that has not previously used for anything else. It also states that one could mix spices into the wax, which would be herbs and incenses agreeable to the planet.

A very potent spirit seal or lamen can thus be fashioned from one of the mixtures mentioned in the list of lamens or incenses of this book and blended with new wax and perhaps a wax color suitable to the planet. Such a lamen would be a potent spirit seal indeed! Caution must be used though, as wax seals can easily break or melt if not handled properly. Again, take heed to the instructions for this as *The Magus* states that *this lamen ought to be composed when the moon is in her increase, on the days and hours which agree to the spirit.*

Whether you decide on silver, calfskin parchment, wax, or one of the seven planetary metals, you'll have plenty of magical mediums to explore. My own lamens are designed in accordance to what is illustrated in *The Magus* with additional geometric boarders. I created both parchment and metallic seals for each of the planetary Archangels. Illustrations of all seven seals are given below, along with further corresponding materials which may be used in their construction. Use a measure of intuition, wisdom, and creativity to create your lamen. Remember to keep it safe and worn only for the DSIC operations, at least initially. As with the vestments, a blessing/

consecration for the Lamen is not mentioned in DSIC, but is given in *A Complete Book of Magic Science*, which you will find below:

Benediction of the Lamens:

O God Thou God of my Salvation, I call upon Thee by the mysteries of Thy most holy Name, On, St. Agla, I worship and beseech Thee by Thy names El, Elohim, Elohe, Zebaoth, and by Thy Mighty Name Tetragrammaton, Saday, that Thou wilt be seen in the power and force of these Thy most holt names so written filling them with divine virtue and Influence through Jesus Christ our Lord.

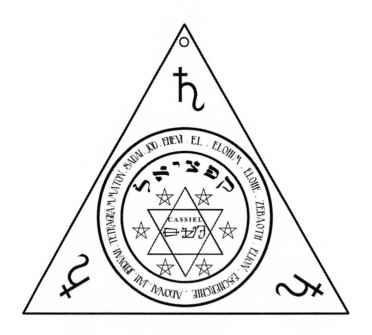

Cassiel –Saturn

Number: 3

Appropriate Materials: Lead, Parchment, *Silver*, Wax, Granite, Jet, Lodestone, Onyx

Color: Black

Ingredients (Wax lamen): Aconite, Alder, Cumin, Cypress, Datura, Pine, Yew, Rue, Belladonna, Coltsfoot, Deadly Nightshade, Henbane, Houseleek, Ivy, Hemlock, Wolfsbane

Sachiel –Jupiter

Number: 4

Appropriate Materials: Tin, Parchment, *Silver*, Wax, Amethyst, Lapis Lazuli, Sapphire, Sugilite, Tuthia

Color: Royal Blue/Purple

Ingredients (Wax lamen): Anise, Ash, Buttercup, Carnation, Coltsfoot, Cinnamon, Dogwood, Lilacs, Hyssop, Narcissus, Heliotrope, Lobelia, Nutmeg, Oak, Opium Poppy, Plum, Poplar, Peony, Valerian, Chestnut, Fig, Juniper

ഇ൝ ൙ന

Samael – Mars

Number: 5

Appropriate Materials: Iron, Parchment, *Silver*, Wax, Ruby, Lodestone, Steel

Color: Red

Ingredients (Wax lamen): Acacia, Arum, Cedar, Hawthorn, Holly, Thistle, Monkshood, Thorn, Cardamom, Daisy, Devil's Claw Root, Stinging Nettle, Poppy, Pepper-tree, Plantain, Rue, Thistle, Thyme, Wormwood, Woodbine

ഇ൝ ൙ന

℘ ℘

Michael –Sun

Number: 6

Appropriate Materials: Lead, Parchment, Silver, Wax, Gold, Citrine

Color: Gold, Yellow

Ingredients (Wax lamen): Orange, Angelica, Acacia, Bay, Chicory, Sunflower, Lovage, Marigold, Heliotrope, Hibiscus, Hops, Rowan, Peony, Marigold

℘ ℘

Anael–Venus

Number: 7

Appropriate Materials: Copper, Parchment, Silver, Wax, Carnelian, Coral, Emerald, Aetites, Rose Quartz

Color: Green

Ingredients (Wax lamen): Blackberry, Black Cherry, Gooseberry, Pomegranate, Strawberry, Carnation, Delphiniums, Damiana, Fennel, Honeysuckle, Jasmine, Myrtle, Rose, Tansy, Verbena

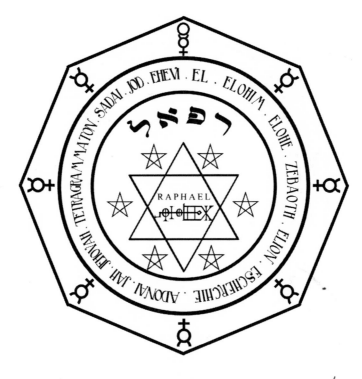

Raphael – Mercury

Number: 8

Appropriate Materials: Fixed Mercury, Parchment, *Silver*, Wax, Cinnabar, Alloys

Color: Orange, Mixed Colors

Ingredients (Wax lamen): Hazel Nut, Larch, Mulberry, Rowan, Caraway, Cinquefoil, Dill, Fennel, Fenugreek, Fern, Lavender, Clover, Marjoram, Matricaria, Maidenhair Fern, Yarrow, Valerian

Gabriel —Moon

Number: 9

Appropriate Materials: Silver, Parchment, Wax, Aquamarine, Clear Quartz, Fluorite, Geodes, Moonstone or Pearls

Color: Silver

Ingredients (Wax lamen): Coconut Palm, Alum Root, Chickweed, Camphor, Iris, Morning Glory, Rampion, Passionflower, Peonies, Poppy, Purslane, Reed, Weeping Willow

THE BOOK OF SPIRITS OR LIBER SPIRITUUM

The infamous Book of Spirits is the archetypical book of magic, which has captured the imagination of the esoteric western world. More than a grimoire, this is the tome depicted in classical portrayals of spirit conjuration. Sometimes one and the same, the Book of Spirits is an activated instrument for the conjuring of spirits, whereas the grimoire, or *grammar* of magic, can be simply a recipe or how-to book.

The *Liber Spirituum*, depicted in classical drawings and popular media, typically shows a magician gazing at an open book while a spirit (usually a demon) appears to their horror and fascination.

The Book of Spirit's true form and function has fascinated me for years. The idea of possessing a book which holds the very essence of the spirits pictured within was too much to resist. Very little in the way of clear example or instruction exists which explains how it is made and used. There are a few sources we can look to in order to get a basic idea concerning how one of these might be constructed. For the most complex and detailed instructions on the creation of such a book, we must refer to the texts of *Key of Solomon* and the *Fourth Book of Occult Philosophy,* which also has references as to the creation and usage of this magical book. For a classic example, the first book of *Lemegeton,* called the *Goetia,* is probably the closest example of what a historic *Liber Spirituum* may have looked like. What are omitted are any images or depictions of the spirits.

For our purposes, we will be drawing from instructions given in *the Fourth Book of Occult Philosophy* and from the text of DSIC itself. Inspection reveals that the one has most likely been drawn from the other. The references in both are somewhat vague, but with comparison, a more complete picture is formed. At the end of this section, I have also included the consecration ceremonies found in *Key of Solomon* for further considerations.

The text says that the Book of Spirits should be made of white vellum or (virgin) white paper. If you are unable to create or buy a book of vellum parchment, I suggest using a blank journal of the highest quality, acid-free, unused paper you are able to afford.

To assist you in creating your own Book of Spirits, I am including instructions of how I created my *'Libre Spirituum In De septum Secundeis'* below. The entire process is quite involved and delicate. Penning the book and filling it with all needed conjurations and prayers, plus pages for the spirits, will indeed require much labor.

First, I purchased a board of thin wood, which was cut to 11"x7". From this, I cut two 7"x5" pieces and a strip 7" x.75" for the book spine. All the pieces were sanded smooth and given a light treatment of consecration oil. Trithemius says the Book of Spirits is to be "seven inches long." Seven is the number of planets, and more precisely, the number of planetary angels mentioned in DSIC. Five is the number of Hermetic elements and points of the pentacle, so the symbolic magical equation seemed perfect for a Book of Spirits.

I used a generous amount of red calfskin for the book binding. The leather was cut to 9"x14" and I had plenty left to spare.

The cut wood pieces were adhered to the underside of the cut leather using a hot glue gun. There was approximately an inch of leather around each of the wood boards and about a quarter of an inch left on between either sides of the spine. Next, the edges and corners of the leather were glued around the wood to keep the binding firmly in place.

I purchased a separate journal rather inexpensively which had suitable paper for my needs. The pages were already 7"x5" and made of acid-free, white paper. I gently removed the grouped pages from this journal and attached it to my own journal. I did this by gluing the spine of the page booklet to the wooden spine of my book and then gluing the front and back cover sheets to the front and back pieces of wood. I believe you can also buy separate book page inserts from stores.

After gluing the pages firmly within the binding, I cut two pieces of fine card stock and pasted them to the inside front and back covers. I found a clasp and added it to keep my book safe and secure when not in use. The clasp was made by attaching a 1"x5" strip of the same leather to the back of the book and adding the clasps where they could lock at the front. After the main construction of the book was done, I decided to adorn it with appropriate seals and symbols.

In essence, the Book of Spirits, or *Liber Spirituum*, is a secure journal of all the prayers, invocations, seals, hours, and sigils of the spirits whose places and spheres are known. It may also contain records of new or unknown spirits to be contacted and recorded, all for the sake of calling them up with ease at later times. In 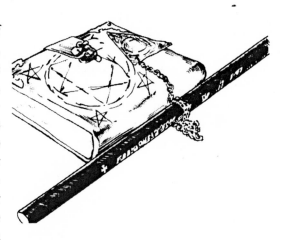 the example that is given in DSIC (in this case, for the Archangel of the Sun, Michael), the author presents an outline of questions that shows how to interrogate and question a conjured spirit. These questions should be recorded somewhere in the beginning pages of your Book of Spirits. They are asked each time to a summed spirit to ensure you are speaking to the correct and intended being.

From the recommendation of the *Fourth Book*, I first adorned my *Liber Spirituum* with the grand Seal (hexagram) of Solomon, which is shown in the *Heptameron* on the front and the triangular seal which is pictured on page 106 of *The Magus*. I also inscribed the front and back bindings with various planetary sigils, a hexagram and pentagram and a seal that includes holy names of the seven planetary angels. Whatever your creative inspiration and use for this item may be, just remember to always treat it as a sacred, magical object.

After you are successful in completing a DSIC operation and able to get the angel to ascribe their oath and symbol within your Book of Spirits, you must be careful to never open the book and flip through it nonchalantly. Although your magical book will undergo updating and addition often, the pages reserved for the spirits (those containing their image, seal, and symbols) should not be opened unless you are purposefully trying to contact them.

I knew these rules beforehand as it is alluded to in the *Fourth Book*, but did not initially adhere to them as closely as I should have. After my first operations, I drew the spirit's image on the selected page of my book and placed my parchment lamen within, as well. I became fascinated with my drawing and would flip to it while entering further information of successive evocations. When I absently gazed at the picture, I got a swift headache and a pulling sensation in my abdomen. The feelings were quite sudden and uncomfortable. It took two more instances of forgetting not to do this until I became convinced of the book's potency. I then made conscious steps to avoid this occurrence in the future. I was amazed by how much of a direct contact the book is to the spirits. When a veritable Book of Spirits is truly active, the spirit really is accessed where its image and sigil is.

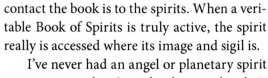

I've never had an angel or planetary spirit pop out at me when I accidently turned to their page, but the physical reminders of their presence coming into awareness with mine was enough to take precaution. I was not mentally and physically prepared for them, so the sudden occurrence caused uncomfortable sensations. I didn't take my reactions as an attack by the spirits, but was convinced the images and seals were powerfully charged and not to be handled or gazed upon idly. Unintentional influences from these beings have the potential to be unsettling at best and dangerously unbalancing at worst. The *Fourth Book of Occult Philosophy* also warns us that our *Liber Spirituum* may lose its potency if handled carelessly or left open and unsecured:

Which book being so written, and well bound, is to be adorned, garnished, and kept secure, with Registers and Seals, lest it should happen after the consecration to open in some place not intended [sic], and indanger [endanger] the operator. Furthermore, this book ought to be kept as reverently as may be: for irreverence of minde causeth it to lose its vertue, with pollution and profanation.

The reality of the possible issues that could arise with this potent, magical tool became strongly apparent, so I decided to add a safeguard against the spirit's pages accidently falling open unintentionally while creating new records: Firstly, whenever I open my *Liber Spirituum*, I make sure to flip to the back page and read the prayer located there. This is the prayer that begins with "AIN SOPH," which is described in *Key of Solomon*. I designed a simple envelope out of a folded piece of new parchment paper. I then drew the same protective seals as I did on the inside of the book covers. The envelope parchment slips onto the collected pages of about three spirits. I use a few to keep the completed spirit pages secure with no chance of them falling open while I'm recording new spirits in or out of an operation. The paper envelope seems to work well and I haven't had further incident of calling up unintended presences. The experience left me with a newfound respect for the *Liber Spirtiuum* and its effective use in not only recording, but calling up spirits with ease!

My *Book of Spirits* with closing hasp

CONSECRATION OF THE BOOK. From *VERTIBLE KEY OF SOLOMON:*

*Make a small Book containing the Prayers for all the Operations, the Names of the Angels in the form of Litanies, their Seals and Characters; the which being done thou shalt consecrate the same unto God and unto the pure Spirits in the manner following:—Thou shalt set in the destined place a small table covered with a white cloth, whereon thou shalt lay the **Book opened at the Great Pentacle which should be drawn on the first leaf of the said Book;***

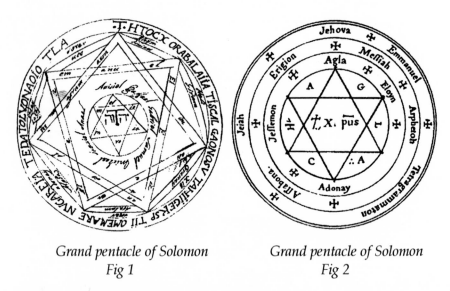

Grand pentacle of Solomon
Fig 1

Grand pentacle of Solomon
Fig 2

The method for using the Book of Spirits described in *The Art of Drawing Spirits into Crystals* is explained below:

> *…take out thy little book, which must be made about seven inches long, of pure white virgin vellum or paper, likewise pen and ink must be ready to write down the name, character and office, likewise the seal or image of whatever spirit may appear (for this, I must tell you that it does not happen that the same spirit you call will always appear, for you must try the spirit to know whether he be a pure or impure being, and this thou shalt easily know by a firm and undoubted faith in God).*

You will notice a similarity between the format described above and the way each of the planetary Archangels are presented in the section where I introduce them. This was done intentionally and should serve as an example of how the main pages of the Book of Spirits should appear. A bit later, the text describes how this book is to be used when the evoked being successfully appears before you:

> *(Here let him (the spirit) swear, then write down his seal or character in thy book, and against it, his office and times to be called, through God's name; also write down anything he may teach thee, or any*

responses he may make to thy questions or interrogations, concerning life or death, arts or sciences, or any other thing;)

It is best if all this information is recorded during the ritual, as you or your scryer receive the answers from the spirits during the interrogation portion of the process. If you have separate sheets of paper with you, you can use those to record the information first, and then add it to the book afterward. Another option is to use a pencil during the ritual, review it, and go over it permanently in ink afterward.

In the *Fourth Book of Occult Philosophy*, we are given a bit more detail as to what the *Liber Spirituum* might look like and to what ends it may be utilized. It's highly probable that the DSIC operation influenced or was influenced by the directions given in the above mentioned work. The descriptions seem to match significantly and the usage of both described books is in direct correlation of one another. Notice the similar construction and inclusion of the spirits name and offices below:

Now, this book is to be made of most pure and clean paper that has never been used before; which many do call Virgin-paper. And this book must be inscribed after this manner: that is to say, Let there be placed on the left side the image of the spirit, and on the right side his character, with the Oath above it, containing the name of the spirit, and his dignity and place, with his office and power. Yet very many do compose this book otherwise, omitting the characters or image: but it is more efficacious not to neglect anything which conduceth to it.

Moreover, there is to be observed the circumstances of places, times, hours, according to the Stars which these spirits are under, and are seen to agree unto, their site, rite, and order being applied. Which book being so written, and well bound, is to be adorned, garnished, and kept secure, with Registers and Seals, lest it should happen after the consecration to open in some place not intended [sic], and endanger the operator. Furthermore, this book ought to be kept as reverently as may be: for irreverence of mind causes it to lose its virtue, with pollution and profanation.

Now, this sacred book being this composed according to the manner already delivered, we are then to proceed to the consecration thereof

*after a twofold way: one whereof is, That every spirit which is written in
the book, are to be called to the Circle, according to the Rites and Order
which we have before taught; and the book that is to be consecrated, let
there be placed without the Circle in a triangle.*

In the case of our experiment, the book is kept within the circle for the
first encounter in which the magician or scryer records the image and symbols of the spirit in question. At the second successful evocation, the book
may be set upon the altar where the Holy Table and ebony pedestal rests. If
no room is allotted for this, it would be customary to lay it on the floor (possibly within a drawn triangle) before the Holy Table. It is also important for
your book to be able to lay flat on its own with the correct pages open to the
section relevant to the spirit being summoned.

*And in the first place, let there be read in the presence of the spirits all
the oaths/prayers/invocations which are written in that book; and then
the book to be consecrated being placed without the Circle in a triangle
there drawn, let all the spirits be compelled to impose their hands where
their images and characters are drawn, and to confirm and consecrate
the same with a special and common Oath. Which being done, let the
book be taken and shut, and preserved as we have before spoken, and
let the spirits be licensed to depart, according to due rite and order.*

The Holy Table already has a triangle upon it, but that is not to say another couldn't be formed on the ground. Chalk, cloth, rope, or impressions
drawn on the ground could be made around your Holy Table beyond the
circle. This could be utilized for consecrating the Book of Spirits or other
talismans you might wish to empower.

*But the Operator, when he would work by the book thus consecrated,
let him do it in a fair and clear season, when the spirits are least
troubled.*

The *Goetia* also speaks of the importance of evoking spirits in "clear
weather." Besides the hour and day, the weather and phase of the moon
should also be taken into consideration and recorded in your experiments.

... and let him place himself towards the region of the spirits. Then let him open the book under a due Register (open to a blank page in the section which is reserved for the particular planetary intelligence you are trying to contact.); let him invoke the spirits by their Oath there described and confirmed, and by the name of their character and image, to that purpose which you desire: and, if there be need; conjure them by the bonds placed in the end of the book. And having attained your desired effect, then you shall license the spirits to depart.

The intended prayers for the planet are specifically those listed in the *Heptameron* or *Veritable Key of Solomon*. These could refer to special invocations that a spirit instructs you to use in summoning it. The main invocation used to conjure the spirit in DSIC is used foremost, but the aforementioned prayers could be used in tandem to hasten the spirit along. In your Book of Spirits, these prayers are written on the page just right of the picture of the spirit. *Veritable Key of Solomon* has excellent sets of three prayers for invoking each planetary spirit that could also be included. The above paragraph explains in differing detail the exact operation of the DSIC experiment and how it should be conducted concerning the use of the Book of Spirits. It also suggests that the consecration of the book occurs automatically when the prayers and invocations are recited for the spirit to appear and swear an oath by.

The section below demonstrates how the magician is in fact *invoking* rather than evoking the angels/Archangels of the planetary spheres and ascended Sephirot in order to compel the lesser planetary intelligences or spirits to appear. It is my assessment that the blessings of each of the planet's major angels should be received foremost, before any evocation of subordinate spirits is attempted. In successful performance of these rituals, the magician is integrating the ascended spheres of the seven planets and harmonizing them within him or herself.

Veritable Key of Solomon hints at this occurrence of integration in a section where it declares:

It is necessary also, in the Consecration of the Book, to summon all the Angels who's Names are written therein in the form of Litanies, the which thou shalt do with devotion; and even if the Angels and Spirits appear not in the Consecration of the Book, be not thou astonished thereat, seeing that they are of a pure nature, and consequently have much difficulty in familiarizing themselves with men who are inconstant and impure, but the Ceremonies and Characters being correctly carried out devotedly and with perseverance, they will be constrained to come, and it will at length happen that at thy first invocation thou wilt be able to see and communicate with them. But I advise thee to undertake nothing unclean or impure, for then thy importunity, far from attracting them, will only serve to chase them from thee; and it will be thereafter exceedingly difficult for thee to attract them for use for pure ends.

My experiences with various spirits and angels have led me to believe that these lesser entities may not necessarily be 'evil' in the typical sense of the word. That is to say, "counter to everything beneficial for man." They are instead beings of their own particular nature, which may be chaotic or extreme in regards to the well-being of a person. Do not assume this means any spirit has the best intentions for the magician who conjures them to visible appearance. Understanding comes with experience and direct knowledge of each Archangel must be grasped before experimenting with their lower intelligences. Thus, we have a sound reason why invocations to each of the Archangelic rulers should be made foremost.

I've included the consecration and evocation ritual for the planetary spirits given in *Key of Solomon* below. The procedures do not exactly match the experiment of DSIC as given in *The Magus*, but they give some more ideas on how the *Liber Spirituum* may be further consecrated and utilized:

And having kindled a lamp which should be suspended above the center of the table, thou shalt surround the said table with a white curtain; clothe thyself in the proper vestments, and holding the Book open, repeat upon thy knees the following prayer with great [attention and] humility:—

'ADONAI, ELOHIM, EL, EHEIEH ASHER EHEIEH, Prince of Princes, Existence of Existences, have mercy upon me, and cast Thine eyes upon Thy Servant (N.), who invokes Thee most devotedly, and supplicates Thee by Thy Holy and tremendous Name Tetragrammaton to be propitious, and to order Thine Angels and Spirits to come and take up their abode in this place; O ye Angels and Spirits of the Stars, O all ye Angels and Elementary Spirits, O all ye Spirits present before the Face of God, I

the Minister and faithful Servant of the Most High conjure ye, let God himself, the Existence of Existences, conjure ye to come and be present at this Operation, I, the Servant of God, most humbly entreat ye. Amen.'

After which thou shalt incense it with the incense proper to the Planet and the day, and thou shalt replace the Book on the aforesaid Table, taking heed that the fire of the lamp be kept up continually during the operation, and keeping the curtains closed. Repeat the same ceremony for seven days, beginning with Saturday, and perfuming the Book each day with the Incense proper to the Planet ruling the day and hour, and taking heed that the lamp shall burn both day and night; after the which thou shalt shut up the Book in a small drawer under the table, made expressly for it, until thou shalt have occasion to use it; and every time that thou wishes to use it, clothe thyself with thy vestments, kindle the lamp, and repeat upon thy knees the aforesaid prayer, 'Adonai Elohim.' etc.

It is necessary also, in the Consecration of the Book, to summon all the Angels who's Names are written therein in the form of Litanies, the which thou shalt do with devotion; and even if the Angels and Spirits appear not in the Consecration of the Book, be not thou astonished thereat, seeing that they are of a pure nature, and consequently have much difficulty in familiarizing themselves with men who are inconstant and impure, but the Ceremonies and Characters being correctly carried out devotedly and with perseverance, they will be constrained to come, and it will at length happen that at thy first invocation thou wilt be able to see and communicate with them. But I advise thee to undertake nothing unclean or impure, for then thy importunity, far from attracting them, will only serve to chase them from thee; and it will be thereafter exceedingly difficult for thee to attract them for use for pure ends.

Again, we see it clearly indicated that we are initially *invoking* the higher angels and asking their assistance. This action promotes understanding, if not integration, of the strengths of their offices. The Archangels are not to be forcefully evoked. The above statement really speaks to the purity and patience it takes to communicate properly with these beings. Such undertaking is no small task and requires sincere effort to succeed in any great degree.

THE ALTAR OF THE STARS
(OPTIONAL, AUTHOR-CREATED TOOL)

After I created my ebony wand, pedestal, Holy Table, and book of spirits, I wondered exactly what I would put the scrying arrangement on and what it should look like. Originally, I thought to use one of my other stands, which was already made. However, I thought this art should have its own altar specific to this type of work. After some imagination and inspiration, I came up with a fairly simple design with powerful, symbolic references.

I began by purchasing a plank of wood and I cut it in two equal 12"x24" pieces. I also had a 2"x4" and two 1"x2"s cut to three feet long. All the wood was given a couple coats of ebony stain and allowed to dry for a few days. Afterward, I used a white paint pen and drew out a hexagram within circles for the bottom and top portions of the 12"x24" pieces. I used one for the base and the other with the blank side for the top. On the surface top of the altar, I drew out the Grand Seal of Solomon and two pentacles where the candle sticks would be located. The 2"x4" became the center pillar with the 1"x2" pieces being the side supports. The center pillar was painted on all four sides, with planetary kamea on the front and planetary symbols on the reverse side. The sides of the main pillar were painted with planetary angelic symbols and *Armadel* Olympic spirit sigils. The side supports were done with all twelve zodiac signs in descending order. The top of the altar has all three sets of symbol/sigils for all seven planets painted on its sides and underneath.

The altar turned out to be just the correct height for me to sit and gaze directly into the crystal mounted on the ebony pedestal. It offers plenty of room for the Holy Table and the silver candlesticks on either side. The simple design allows the altar to be moved rather easily and adjusted in the exact position you want. For some of the ceremonies, I used an altar cloth of corresponding planetary color with the Holy Table and candles placed on top. The symbols all correspond to intelligences of the planetary spheres and are geared toward those ends. I could not think of a better altar to use for the experiment of DSIC. I decided that "Altar of the Stars" was an appropriate name and was suited for this piece of magical furniture.

The material used for constructing the altar does not have to be of any specific kind but again I would recommend only using natural materials like stone or wood. I built mine out of simple pine board, which worked perfectly. The stand upon which the Holy Table is set is not mentioned at all in the text. Granted, the Holy Table could be fashioned from a full-sized table or altar itself, which it may have been. Regardless of what you use, be sure it is sturdy, appropriate, and utilized for this particular magical operation only. A stand or large table made entirely of ebony wood sounded appealing at first, but the enormous weight and difficulty I would have in moving it around a room made me change my mind. Pine or a sturdy oak are perfectly adequate materials for an altar. All of my operations have been conducted using my pine Altar of the Stars, and I have had no complaints whatsoever in its suitability.

Alter of the Stars, Top

Altar of the Stars

Complete Altar setup with tripod

THE CIRCLE OF ART AND COMPLETE SETUP

The last, but definitely not the least, piece of furniture for this magical operation I will be covering is the magical circle. No classic grimoire of medieval magic would be complete without the *circle of art,* which is another name for the magic circle. Used not only as an impenetrable wall of defense against potentially hazardous invoked forces, the circle represents the magician's single point of axis in the universe.

Nothing of a mundane nature should ever be done within a magic circle. Once within its boundaries, you are one with your Creator and assume an authoritative position of command and divine/True Will. Countless modern magical works go into the nature and symbolism of the magic circle, so I will try not to regurgitate knowledge that has been explained ample times by other writers. Just as with the wand, and every other piece of magical equipment, you should intrinsically *feel* the associated power of its direct, symbolic representation within you. Otherwise, all you are doing is setting a stage with props.

The circle is the concentrated gathering of the magician's *will,* the device and doorway to connecting with his or her deity and un-defiled true self, in pure expression. Many magical circles, especially those from the *Greater* and *Lesser Keys of Solomon,* are quite large and complex. Typically, the circle's diameter in these grimoires, as well as in *A Complete Book of Magic Science,* is to be nine feet. *"And on the day before, draw the lines of the Circle in a fair place and let the diameter of the innermost circle be nine feet"* (p. 8). *The Heptameron* and *Goetia* also describe a circle that is nine feet across. My first inclination was to have a circle of this same size, but after some experimentation, it seemed impractical, due to the smallness of the scrying device and table of art.

If we assume that the altar and crystal for viewing the spirits is outside the circle, one would have to be crammed near the edge of it to view the crystal properly if they were the only one operating. Nine feet might be an appropriate diameter for two or more people. However, even two people can fit comfortably in a circle of five to seven feet in diameter. I would not recommend having your magic circle be any smaller than five feet across, as it gets difficult to move around and arrange your implements, even with one person. The illustration of the circle, as drawn in the DSIC example, is very simple in design and use. A band containing a hexagram at each of the four cardinal points (or sub quarters, depending on the direction you are facing), plus three divine names of God, and, finally, the symbol and name of the angel you are evoking to your Holy Table. The circle in *A Complete Book of Magic Science* shows a two-ringed enclosure with an interwoven circle on the outside where the spirit is to appear. The main circle features crosses (four in each circle) at the cross quarter points instead of hexagrams. No section is given for the spirit's name or symbols, however. Different holy names also appear on the inside and outside of the circle. The separate circle for the spirit is particularly interesting, as it further supports the idea that the spirit or angel is made to appear outside the magician's circle.

The simplicity of the circle featured in DSIC almost seems suspect when compared with the one mentioned above or the multi-ringed circle of Peter Abino's *Heptameron*. This design uses similar names and symbols, plus the day and hour of the spirit being evoked. I will state here that the *Complete Book of Magic Science* or *Heptameron* circle would seem appropriate to experiment with due to its similar nature to DSIC, but contains different elements which may not support this ritual. Regardless, I opted to use the circle listed in the DSIC section of *The Magus* and have not had any regrets.

It is ideal to have a magical room with a hard floor and draw your circle on it with chalk or blessed charcoal. You could also use paints if you plan on having your circle be permanent. The room should be large enough to accommodate each piece of equipment, plus all people involved in the ritual, comfortably.

An additional feature that I also used during the Almadel experiments was to have a complete canopy enclosure around the operating area I was using. This is not as difficult as it would first seem and simply requires a large metal or wooden hoop with attached draperies of the color of your choice. Be sure it is large enough to allow room for altar and burning candles without it posing a fire hazard.

Another option is to paint or draw your circle on material like canvas or a cloth sheet. This was the method I settled on because the circle is without any inner words or symbols. It was rather easy to construct and quick to paint.

I purchased a 7'x9' tarp, marked the very center, and used a thumb tack, pencil, and string to mark out the circle. The center was found using a tape measure for precision. I then used reinforced duct tape to hold the pin in place and looped the string around it. The pencil was wrapped tightly to the other end of the string and I marked out a seven foot circle. Afterward, I took the pencil a foot in and marked out the width of the circle. The circle was then cut out and given a front and back coating of white latex paint

The section of the circle where the angel's name and sigil are located was left blank. Separate sections were made from strips of canvas to fit on top of the circle, for every angel. You can also use chalk or an erasable instrument to change out the names, if you so choose. The section of the circle with the angel's name and sigil is to be directly in front of your Holy Table, pointed in the direction of the spirit. During my operations, I realized how the proximity of the angel's name and symbols allow its energy to transmit within the circle in a direct, yet controlled manner.

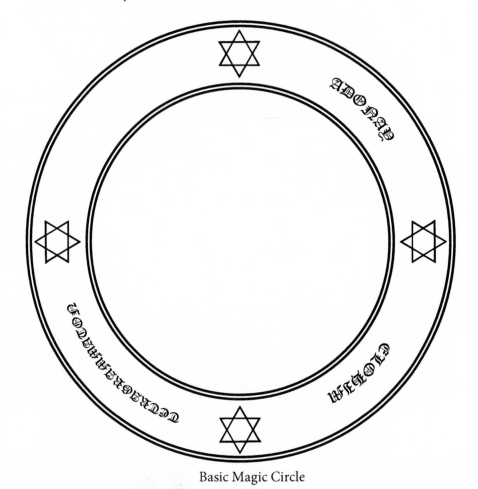

Basic Magic Circle

In my completed circle, I used black paint to boarder the inside and outside of the circle. I also included ancient, as well as traditional, Hebrew characters for the sacred names. This was an inspirational modification on my part, but one that seemed appropriate to fill the space of the circle. I also included the Romanized spelling of the Archangel's name, as well as its Hebrew one. I do not think this is necessary for the strength of the circle, but it felt appropriate for the design. As in all cases of equipment experimentation, I leave it to the discretion of the reader to decide on its final design.

Finished circle with Cassiel spirit section

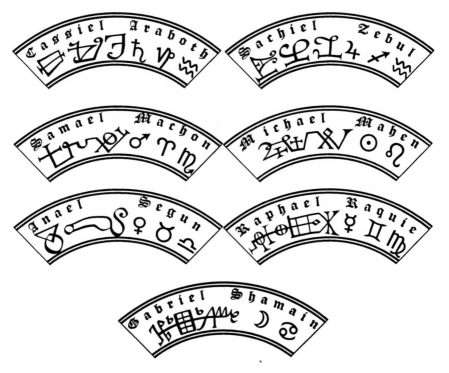

Unless you are accustomed to standing or kneeling for long periods of time, I would consider using something to sit upon for the duration of your experiments. A stool keeps your limbs from falling asleep or becoming cramped. It will also allow the proper eye level for an approximately three foot high table with the scrying device on top of it. If you are working with a scryer, they should be seated while you operate standing behind them. If you find it too tiresome to stand for the duration of the ceremony, both of you could be seated on separate stools.

Even though there is no mention of one in the text, I find that a separate small table or stand can also be helpful to have with you in the circle. Such a table is convenient for holding all of the ritual items needed for the ceremony, such as the Book, wand, ring and lamen. The ebony pedestal should also be placed here for the initial blessing. If you do not have a table or not enough room within your circle, you can use your stool as a small table while kneeling in front of it.

A white linen or colored altar cloth covering for your chair and perhaps matching your robe is a nice addition. The tripod censor should be just beyond your circle, in front of the altar and in the proper direction of the spirit. When seated, the altar should appear fairly close in front of you just beyond the censor. You should be able to gaze directly at your crystal sphere within the ebony pedestal with ease. In no way should you feel cramped or near to passing your limbs outside the boarder of your protective circle.

Other magicians who have experimented with this system place the altar and scrying device *within* the magic circle. I considered this option at length, but settled on viewing the crystal outside the circle. The decision for placing the tripod and the Holy Table outside of the circle was from the section of DSIC which reads, *"Then place the vessel for the perfumes **between** thy circle and the holy table on which the crystal stands…"* The author could have meant within the circle behind the Holy Table, but it didn't seem to fit. I speculated that it was the size of the circle and proximity of the Holy Table that makes the ultimate difference.

During an operation, I sit near the edge of the circle with the section that has the spirit's sigil, name, and symbols. The tripod is directly in front of the circle and beneath the view of the crystal. The crystal is no more than a foot and a half away and easy to gaze at directly. The table that holds my ritual equipment is located at my right and easily accessible. This setup could also work with a seer sitting directly in the front with enough space for the Operator/magus to conjure from behind. I prefer this arrangement also when evoking lesser intelligences or potentially dangerous spirits. I am not against the idea of having the altar and Holy Table within the circle, but I have not personally tried it, so I cannot say how well it works. Dr. Dee and Edward Kelly contacted the Enochian angels within a sacred space, so this art could potentially work in a similar fashion. Again, I cannot say what the potential drawbacks or benefits might be. I leave it up to the reader as another option to try.

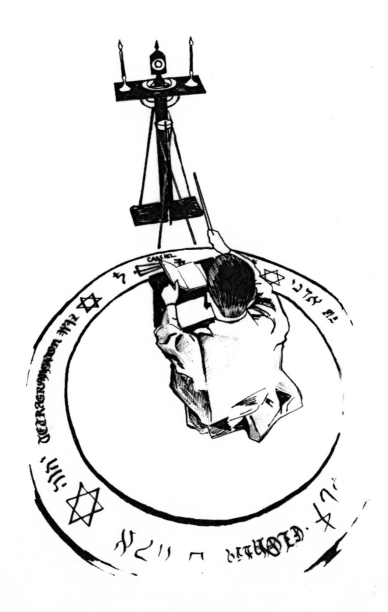

WORKSPACE OF THE MAGICIAN

There has been much debate and literature written on the subject of the magical room, temple, chamber, or oratory. Often, authors of the past have done their best to appeal to the "magician on a budget" and describe methods for transforming a bedroom or living room into a temporary magical or sacred space. As difficult as this may be for many readers, I cannot condone this method, as the differences I've seen while working in such a space as compared to my magical rooms set aside for just such experiments are incomparable. For the dedication, time, energy, and effort needed to reconstruct the experiment I describe in this work, a magical room should be a priority.

The magical room should be unobstructed and internally free from any sort of visual or auditory distractions, such as exterior light, passersby, objects, people looking in windows, loud street noises, etc. Nothing of a mundane nature should be done in this area, so ideally, a room separate from day-to-day affairs should be reserved for this type of working only. There needn't be any fancy decoration or magical artifacts in the room besides the ones you will be using expressly for the DSIC experiment. A large chest or cabinet to keep your ritual implements stored and secure would be appropriate. Conduct only serious spiritual and magical operations in this room; whether you are cleaning, preparing, organizing, or contemplating future operations, all should be done with a reverent state of mind and being. I cannot remember if it was due to my study of the *Book of Abramelin the Mage*, but I also do not enter my magical chamber wearing shoes. I either will go barefoot or only wear shoes intended as part of the magical vestments, such as the ones described in *Key of Solomon*. In my DSIC experiments, I do not wear any shoes. In following chapters, I will explain individual purifications to prepare for traditional magical workings. I will also explain preparing magical working space.

If working with a scryer, I would recommend the two of you take enough time individually to prepare for the work. Conduct the purification process separately and arrange for a time before the ceremony to regroup. Purification is a very important prerequisite to traditional evocation of any sort and especially when attempting to contact angelic beings. In today's society, all too often, the busy magician neglects this magical practice in anticipation of getting right to spirit interaction. The truth of the matter is that such correspondences will either not take place successfully or not be integrated possibly without the ritually purified mind, body, and will.

THE PURIFICATION

The effects of purification rites, conscious affirmations of abstaining from a variety of luxuries, pleasures and cravings, as well as day-to-day habits, are multifold. In conjunction with the act of bathing and anointing ourselves with oil, we are purifying our bodies through all the senses. You'll find many, if not most, religious and spiritual practices around the world have long lasting traditions of fasting and purifying oneself to reach spiritual ends.

As modern practitioners of spiritual, mystical and cultural arts, we can actually view these actions and their benefits in a variety of ways. First, we have noticeable changes both physically and mentally for consciously choosing new modes of behavior action and self-denial.

As modern practitioners of spiritual, mystical, and cultural arts, we can actually view these actions and their benefits in a variety of ways. First, we have noticeable changes both physically and mentally for consciously choosing new modes of behavior, action, and self-denial.

As a wise man once said, "The most powerful thing we can do as humans is to tell ourselves, 'No.'" To deny certain habits, cravings, distractions, and unconscious preoccupations is an act of self-mastery and empowerment.

Instead of letting our wants and cravings rule us, we make conscious efforts to choose what we do and how we act down to every detail. Retreat is a very powerful practice that is found in all places in the world and a lifestyle chosen by many religious and spiritual leaders/teachers around the world. Being able to purify ourselves and go without is to acknowledge that those "things" do not control us, but we control them. Also, we begin to pay close(r) attention and control various actions and habits we might otherwise let go unnoticed.

In the Western magick tradition, as well as many eastern ones, demons seem to love vice and enjoy encouraging all manner of disabling and un-empowering actions in people in order to take power away from them. Angels, on the other hand, seem to respect humility and those who are genuine and pure. Whether or not you believe or adhere to this idea is beside the point. People who have no sense of self control or actualization tend to be the criminals or both mentally and emotionally crippled. Few powerful people will argue that letting one's every whim and desire go unchecked is a good way to live. Lazy people make excuses and justifications for most things they do or don't do in life and what happens to them, while the powerful make who they want to be.

The ritual purification process is both physically and emotionally taxing. It rips one away from their normal, comfortable routines and forces them to take conscious control of every part of their functioning. I believe this is essential for magical success in the larger scheme of things and also very necessary for certain rites of evocation and spiritual contact. It's a very pointed *discipline*. The process of purification is a key ingredient to actually being able to perform a successful evocation and connect properly to the divine. For the magician, it's showing alignment to God/The Divine, mastery of the self, and control over one's "universe." It's making a conscious decision to trial the body in order to strengthen the spirit.

Persons who have no sense of discipline have no sense of real personal power, plain and simple. This is unfortunately a difficult realization for many westerners in this day and age. Obesity is a perfect result and example of a lack of personal power in favor of satiating wants and cravings. I personally have difficulty believing anyone who makes claims to personal power while having no control over their own health, wealth, habits, and cravings.

Restricting or changing the usual diet encourages the body and mind to function differently. Over the years, I have learned this must be done specifically to the body of the magician, so as not to cause "weakness" (malnourishment) or other disabling factors that would inhibit rather than help magical efforts. However, serious efforts should be taken to adhere to the prescriptions of the grimoires (if that is what you are doing), as cutting any corners out of personal weakness, laziness, or aversion to change will not aid a magical act in any way.

The purification process should cause a noteworthy "disturbance" of change within the magician to such a degree that his or her mind is literally ripped from the padded enclosure of the safely habitual life. It exposes the raw senses of conscious living which, for the gifted, opens up new realms of perceptions, insights, and comprehension, the ideal space for spirit-human interaction. You will notice a direct shift in your thought process and awareness.

Many shamans, holy men, and, sometimes, lay people will become initiated into their gifts through traumas. Sometimes severe illness, near death episodes, or something which causes the person to step into the otherworld and return to tell about it will cause this shift of consciousness. The purification process, along with fasting and self-denial, is a method of entering into this nebulous space of existence in order to communicate clearly with spiritual beings. Shifting our habits and perceptions is a direct way to speak with those who do not support the typical way of logical interaction and physical relationship.

As far as the baths, prayers, and scented oils/incense go, many spirits seem to appreciate cleanliness and centeredness, which is amplified by the removal of conscious and unconscious distractions. For the magician, the mind will reach a point which makes concentration and determination — will — not only possible, but extremely heightened in potency. In the realm of the grimoires, the cleanliness is a movement toward God (godhead) ascension.

You must have an active participation and control over your inner workings (microcosm) to seriously achieve anything in the outer world (macrocosm). Prayer, intense fasting, isolation, and denial are traditional ways to bring the mind and will into very powerful focus. Anyone who chooses to undergo such a trial for the sake of achieving magical ends will definitely be determined in seeing those ends accomplished! It is not enough to simply have the equipment and furniture and perform a well-rehearsed ritual with moderate amounts of enthusiasm, energy, and will. This is why *many* have still not experienced what these arts and books have to offer. Very few have the discipline to even complete the purification process, let alone the entire ritual itself.

To better understand the elements of the purification process, simply look at what is involved and the means behind them:

WATER: The conduit, the essential life element, the realm of the unconscious . . . seen to many as the *otherworld*. Many do not know this, but the ancient Jewish people, as well as many other cultures, viewed the sea and deep waters as the realm of the dead, otherworld, and, sometimes, hell itself. To immerse yourself in water and reemerge is a direct symbolic act of rebirth, returning from the otherworld and being reborn in newness. It helps if the sincere ritual of baptism is apprehended and relearned beyond the dogmatic understanding of the modern western church. Holy water is used to asperse people, places, and things, namely the ritual areas and ritual implements before a magical ceremonial operation.

FASTING: Taking energy away from the body and physical senses in favor of bringing forth energy and power from an alternate source. Also, through fasting, we are ridding ourselves of chemical and toxin stores. A literal physical cleansing will lessen unpleasant odors and empty the bowels. It will also alter or brain functions and cause perceptions to change.

PRAYER: Connecting to one's deity. To God. To be mentally, spiritually, and emotionally "clean" by confessing and acknowledging any wrongdoings, freeing ourselves from guilt and any mental/emotional blockages that may either be unacknowledged or buried deep. To step into full affirmation that whatever magical act you intend to perform is in agreement with divine authority, totality, and the working intelligence of the universe. Letting go of our self-proclaimed righteousness and knowledge of our place in the universe, despite any ill-favored views of religious or spiritual dogmas. This is something that must be intensely personal and truthful, taking place within the consciousness of the magician.

RETREAT/MEDITATION: The removal of physical, social, and entertaining distractions and comforts to force one to focus on internal workings and energies, which are typically made invisible by the constructs of mass human interactions. When complete dedication is given to performing the ritual at hand and the self is removed from the day-to-day distractions, much can be accomplished.

OIL/INCENSE: This is not used for merely enticing or exciting the sense of smell. In this case, it is used to uplift the personage of the magician and bring in a sense of sacredness, holiness and appeal to the spiritual realm. (This is assuming that the strong body odors and other earthly senses, like rotting foods, were unappealing to spiritual beings and agents of the divine, etc.)

On closing of this quick summary, any serious magician should refer to the *Book of Abramelin the Mage*. The majority of the magic and the most intense process... indeed, the entire ritual is based on the practice of ritual purification overall. The dealing with angelic and other beings is secondary to the purification process and aligning yourself firmly and dynamically with *sacred action* and, thusly, to the creator. Magicians who sidestep this hugely important ritual step are kidding themselves and will most likely achieve very little in their spiritual progression.

CHAPTER VI

PUTTING IT TO PRACTICE: THE
STEPS FOR EVOCATION

n this section, I cover the entire process of what drawing a spirit into a crystal looks like from beginning to end. As I previously mentioned, a few elements have been added or integrated where there seems to be a common trend among the grimoires. Again, these are based off of my personal assessments after working from various grimoires over the years.

The obvious first step is to decide which spirit you are going to summon. Ask yourself what you are hoping the spirit can do for you and to what ends you will put its information or office. The obvious, yet more important questions you may want to ask yourself are why you are deciding to call this spirit and what your true motivations are.

As far as what is appropriate to ask and converse about, the Invocation to the spirit deals with this directly. You may want to review the Invocation and meditate on it a bit before jumping into the ceremony and asking for something you're not entirely sure you want. This is crucial and may determine if you are ultimately successful or not.

When the spirit is decided upon, you must also know its proper day and hour of calling. The spirit's lamen or seal should have already been made on a previous day and time appropriate to them, as well as the incense mixture you will be using. This may take a bit of work and one should not rush through these vital, preparatory steps. Be sure to answer the "who, what, when, where, and why" questions honestly and completely before moving any further. This should be the rule for any large magical undertaking.

Before acts of traditional ritual magic, there is typically a determined period of retreat and abstinence which was already discussed earlier. This preparatory stage of purification is in agreement with just about every popular grimoire that exits. I will leave the extent and the intensity of this stage to the discretion of the mage.

If we are to again refer to *A Complete Book of Magic Science*, the work states that we are to *"Retire thyself seven days free from all company and fast and pray from sunrise to sunset. Rise every morning at seven of the clock and the three days previous to the work fast upon bread and water."*

In this day, such retreats are difficult and near impossible for many. Personally, I believe no sooner than three hours before the ritual should any meal be eaten or any other activity which is non-congruent to the ritual be undertaken. In texts, such as *Key of Solomon*, a few months or as little as nine days are spent in abstinence, retreat, fasting, prayer, and purification. For an excellent description and guide through the traditional Solomonic bath and fast, see Aaron Leitch's *Secrets of the Magickal Grimoires*. This book is of tremendous value for any magician seriously considering practicing Medieval and early Renaissance magic by the book. This time is best used for getting in touch with the divinity which exists simultaneously within and without you, shedding thoughts and feelings that do not resonate with absolute divinity and focusing solely on the task you are about to perform.

The next part should be the arrangement of the equipment, furniture, and implements that will be used in the ceremony. Have a checklist like the one shown here and make sure you have everything ready ahead of time:

1. Have all pertinent equipment ready within your magical room: Table of Art (Altar of the Stars), crystal in ebony pedestal, wand, tripod, incense, lamen, ring, Book of Spirits, candles and silver candlesticks, invocations, and separate pen and paper for writing down information learned from the spirits, circle, robe, stole, and belt.

2. Use a compass, or any device that gives exact directional coordinates, to locate the proper direction for the spirit.

3. Set your Altar of the Stars, or stand with the Holy Table, at the far end of the direction the angel (or spirit) is to appear. Arrange the candlesticks and candles on both sides.

4. Do not set your pedestal with the crystal ball on the Holy Table yet; keep it in the circle, along with your other tools, for the time being. Also, be sure your circle has the section where the spirit's symbol and sigil are, facing directly in front of the Holy Table.

After you have decided upon your planetary angel or spirit to summon, and you have made certain that your day and hour for the working are favorable, take one more moment to review. Be sure all is correct to the corresponding nature of the angel, and have in readiness all the equipment and materials necessary for your operation. When you and your scryer (if you have one) feel ready, it's time to finally conduct *The Art of Drawing Spirits into Crystals.*

At the beginning of the designated hour and after your preliminary cleansing and fasting, step within the circle and take a moment to center and focus. If someone is accompanying you, both of you should be cleansed and dressed in similar attire with the lamen of the spirit close at hand. When you feel ready to begin, kneel near the crystal in your pedestal and turn your eyes to the heavens. Recite the prayer that is given in the text. (If working with a partner, both should be in a praying position.) Before beginning the actual evocation and call to the spirit, Trithemius says to first recite this prayer and oration unto God:

Oh, God! who art the author of all good things, strengthen, I beseech thee, thy poor servant, that he may stand fast, without fear, through this dealing and work; enlighten, I beseech thee, oh Lord! the dark understanding of thy creature, so that his spiritual eye may be opened to see and know thy angelic spirits descending here in this crystal.

At this point, place both hands over the crystal in an act of blessing and consecration and say:

and thou, oh inanimate creature of God, be sanctified and consecrated, and blessed to this purpose, that no evil phantasy may appear in thee; or, if they do gain ingress into this creature, they may be constrained to speak intelligibly, and truly, and without the least ambiguity, for Christ's sake. Amen.

Take a moment to feel the holy light of God descend upon you (and your scryer, if one is present) and your crystal within the pedestal. Fully realize that this instrument is to be your direct medium of angelic communication. When you are finished, slowly but deliberately place the pedestal in the center of the triangle on your Holy Table. Then, light both candles and return to the center of your circle. Center yourself and resume with the prayer below:

And forasmuch as thy servant here standing before thee, oh, Lord! desires neither evil treasures, nor injury to his neighbor, nor hurt to any living creature, grant him the power of descrying those celestial spirits or intelligences, that may appear in this crystal, and whatever good gifts (whether the power of healing infirmities, or of imbibing wisdom, or discovering any evil likely to afflict any person or family, or any other good gift thou mayest be pleased to bestow on me, enable me, by thy wisdom and mercy, to use whatever I may receive to the honor of thy holy name. Grant this for thy son Christ's sake. Amen.

Note: If the classical, Christian prayers are too much of an aversion to your spiritual nature, I would advise constructing a personal prayer ahead of time which matches the above *as closely as possible.* If you are working with another person, make sure BOTH of you are strongly moved and harmonized with every prayer.

At the conclusion of this prayer, place the magic ring on the little finger of your right hand and then place the lamen around your neck. Again, a separate table within the circle with all the tools placed ahead of time is extremely useful. This table need not be very large and should not be used for any other purpose.

On this table, place the ebony wand, the Book of Spirits, a pen to write with, incense for the tripod censor, matches or other suitable fire making tools, the magic ring, and the lamen. The Book of Spirits should be opened to the page where the spirit's seal and name is drawn. The interrogational questions for the spirit should be written down ahead of time (either in your Book of Spirits or on a separate sheet of paper) with plenty of room for recording any extra information you may learn.

The next section says to consecrate the magical circle and *then* consecrate the incense. This seems most appropriate if you or your scryer is holding the tripod with the perfumes. If this is not the case, you can perform the consecration for the perfumes first and then bless the circle on the floor. However, if you decide to follow the traditional proceedings, have no fear. Once your blessing for the circle is made, it is secure and unbroken by extending past it to place the incense on the coals.

If you are placing the tripod outside your circle, begin by holding your hand or wand a few inches over your censor and extend your concentration to the tripod below. The next step is to light the charcoal for the perfumes, allow it to become red hot, and issue a blessing over it as you light it, saying:

I conjure thee, oh thou creature of fire! by him who created all things both in heaven and earth, and in the sea, and in every other place whatever, that forthwith thou cast away every phantasm from thee, that no hurt whatsoever shall be done in anything. Bless, oh Lord, this creature of fire, and sanctify it that it may be blessed, and that they may fill up the power and virtue of their odors; so neither the enemy, nor any false imagination, may enter into them; through our Lord Jesus Christ. Amen.

Put a generous amount of incense on the charcoal and place the vessel and tripod for the perfumes between your circle and the Holy Table.

After donning your magical equipment, have your ebony wand in your right (or dominant) hand and begin tracing the perimeter of your circle. Begin in the direction of the spirit, moving slowly and steadily clockwise, while saying the below prayer aloud:

In the name of the blessed Trinity, I consecrate this piece of ground for our defense; so that no evil spirit may have power to break these bounds prescribed here, through Jesus Christ our Lord. Amen.

Now comes the moment for the actual Invocation to the spirit. Sit or stand directly in front of your Holy Table where you can gaze into the crystal sphere at a comfortable level. There is no need to strain or stare in a way that causes distraction or discomfort. The incense should be putting out a decent amount of smoke and should be between you and the Holy Table. If, at any time, you need to add more, use your wand or another instrument to pass the circle, but not your hand.

Extend your full focus and concentration toward the crystal and slowly raise your ebony wand vertically before you. When you are ready, intone the below Invocation powerfully and intently. *Vibrating* words in the popular magical lodge method is unnecessary. There is no need to shout or yell, but be firm and fill your voice with focused will.

In the name of the blessed and holy Trinity, I do desire thee, thou strong mighty angel, (name of angel, or any other angel or spirit) that if it be the divine will of him who is called Tetragrammaton. the Holy God, the Father, that thou take upon thee some shape as best becometh thy celestial nature, and appear to us visibly here in this crystal, and answer our demands in as far as we shall not transgress the bounds of the divine mercy and goodness, by requesting unlawful knowledge; but that thou wilt graciously show us what things are most profitable for us to know and do, to the glory and honor of his divine Majesty, who liveth and reigneth, world without end. Amen.

Wait for signs of the spirit's arrival. There should be clear indication and no need to stretch your imagination to fake its presence. Be patient, open, and expectant. If, for some reason, no appearance occurs, continue to this next prayer:

Lord, thy will be done on earth, as it is in heaven; make clean our hearts within us, and take not thy Holy Spirit from us.

To spur the spirit to arrive to your altar quicker, you are to recite the below:

O Lord, by thy name, we have called him, suffer him to administer unto us. And that all things may work together for thy honour and glory, to whom with thee, the Son, and blessed Spirit, be ascribed all might, majesty and dominion. Amen.

The text makes special mention on how to proceed if and when the spirit appears to one or both of you. Again, it reiterates that if you are working with a partner, one of you may perceive the spirit, while the other does not. Be open to this possible occurrence. When a vision manifests, continue on with the prayer below:

Oh, Lord! we return thee our hearty and sincere thanks for the hearing of our prayer, and we thank thee for having permitted thy spirit to appear unto us which we, by thy mercy, will interrogate to our further instruction, through Christ. Amen.

When a spirit arrives and has made itself known, the text has a list of interrogational questions to be put to the spirit that should not be omitted. The operator/magus should record each response directly or from the scryer who is directly conversing with the being.

Question 1: *"In the name of the holy and undefiled Spirit, the Father, the begotten Son, and Holy Ghost, proceeding from both, what is thy true name?"*

Record the perceived answer in the appropriate section of your Book of Spirits, which should be on the right-hand-side page, or else record it on the paper you have with you in the circle.

Question 2: *"What is thy office?"* (Expect possible poetic, symbolic, or metaphorical descriptions here, as angels rarely speak in base terms. They may, but it is rare, in my experience.)

Question 3: *"What is thy true sign or character?"* (Often, after this question is asked, a symbol or image will appear in the crystal which represents the spirit's signature or sign. Sometimes, a new sigil will appear, so be sure to copy it down as accurately as possible.)

Question 4: *"When are the times most agreeable to thy nature to hold conference with us?"* (More often than not, I have received poetic and general replies which deal more with times of the year, certain astrological events, etc.)

Question 5: *"Wilt thou swear by the blood and righteousness of our Lord Jesus Christ, that thou art truly...?"* (I have yet to have an angel hesitate or find this question unappealing.)

> *(Here, let him swear, then write down his seal or character in thy book, and against it, his office and times to be called, through God's name. Also, write down anything he may teach thee, or any responses he may make to thy questions or interrogations, concerning life or death, arts or sciences, or any other thing.)*

It should be mentioned that once you are sure of the angel/spirit's identity, it would be beneficial to ask it many more questions which should have been considered and written down ahead of time. Remember to only ask questions which are pertinent to its office and useful to you. I advise against asking anything trivial or beyond the scope of your comprehension. Angels, especially, appreciate honesty and straightforwardness with the respect that's due them. Do not keep the spirit past its hour of operation and do not hold it longer than is necessary to fulfill your questions. Interactions with beings should be conducted in a respectful and diplomatic fashion with clear intent on behalf of the magician.

When you are finished conversing and questioning the spirit, you should give it formal license to depart by saying:

Thou great and mighty spirit, inasmuch as thou camest in peace and in the name of the ever blessed and righteous Trinity, so in this name thou mayest depart, and return to us when we call thee in his name to whom every knee doth bow down. Fare thee well, (Angel's name); peace be between us, through our blessed Lord Jesus Christ. Amen (Make sign of the cross in the air before you).

The spirit should then depart and when its presence is no longer perceived, you are to say the prayer below:

To God, the Father, eternal Spirit, fountain of Light, the Son, and Holy Ghost, be all honor and glory, world without end. Amen.

This concludes the full operation of Drawing Spirits into Crystals. If you noticed, I added particular steps of my own which I have found to be beneficial for completing this ritual. It goes without saying that each magus may experiment and modify the details, but great caution should be undertaken when doing so.

I hope the explanations and comments in this outline will help many readers in their attempts to perform this ritual for themselves. Once the materials are all constructed and in place, the rest of the procedure is quite simple and straightforward. The extent of what can be learned and accomplished by communicating with these angels is endless. If you are interested in angelic communication, but have apparent blockages for scrying, finding a talented and willing scryer can bring you wonderful results. Invest the effort needed to share this with someone you can trust, someone who will relate their experiences honestly and directly to you, without pretense.

In the next section, I relate my very first experience conducting the DSIC evocation of Archangel Cassiel. The relation is the true record of my first operation and, also, the very beginning of wondrous experiences I would have when performing this magical ritual. As you may have noticed, the lamen and circle section of this angel are featured in many of the illustrations. The reason for this is that the illustrations were done from the only photos taken of my magical implements which I allowed.

All photos were taken shortly after my first evocations. The information below should be considered as an example of how much greater experiences await the tenacious magician who conducts these operations in earnest. I can say with certainty that each consecutive operation was more profound than the last.

CHAPTER VII

AN ACCOUNT OF THE INVOCATION
OF ARCHANGEL CASSIEL

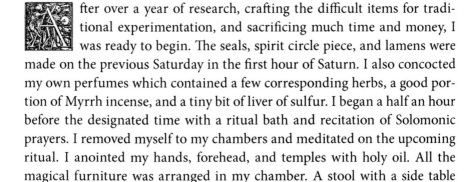fter over a year of research, crafting the difficult items for tradi-
tional experimentation, and sacrificing much time and money, I
was ready to begin. The seals, spirit circle piece, and lamens were
made on the previous Saturday in the first hour of Saturn. I also concocted
my own perfumes which contained a few corresponding herbs, a good portion of Myrrh incense, and a tiny bit of liver of sulfur. I began a half an hour
before the designated time with a ritual bath and recitation of Solomonic
prayers. I removed myself to my chambers and meditated on the upcoming
ritual. I anointed my hands, forehead, and temples with holy oil. All the
magical furniture was arranged in my chamber. A stool with a side table
was set in my circle. On the side table was my lamen, placed within the given
page of my Book of Spirits; my ebony wand; the crystal pedestal; my magic
ring; parchment for writing and recording (along with a pen); a small, lead
box containing the perfumes and charcoal; and holy water. Five minutes
before the hour of Saturn, I sprinkled myself and the circle with holy water,
as well as the walls of the chamber, the ceiling, and the floor.

At the given time, I knelt at the table and lit a central oil lamp that was
set on a table within the circle. The room was quite dark and the lamp was
the only initial source of light. I set the Holy Table on the Altar of the Stars,
re-entered my circle, and knelt once more. I then referred to my Book of
Spirits and recited the opening prayer while I held the ebony pedestal containing the crystal stone as I consecrated it.

Afterward, I set the pedestal on the Holy Table and lit the two black
candles on both sides. I returned to the circle, put on the lead and parchment

lamen, flipped the canvas circle section to show the Saturn sigils, and placed it on the circle. I used my wand to trace the circle, beginning in the North, and recited the *consecration of the circle* as I did. I returned to the center table and opened the box containing the Saturn incense and one piece of coal. I said *the consecration prayer for the fire and incense*, then placed the coal on the tripod and lit it. I placed a portion of the Saturn incense on the coals, and as the smoke rose, I sat and began the main invocation to Cassiel.

During the first recitation of the Invocation, the atmosphere in the room seemed to thicken and I saw a prominent dark figure fill up the entire central circle of the gold disk and the crystal stone. I was initially unsure if this was a manifestation since it did not move, so I continued on with the other invocations. The candle flames grew rigidly still and the figure came into better focus, but did not speak. I gave *the prayer of thanks,* which is given in the text, although it seemed to distract somewhat from what was occurring. The figure didn't move, however, so I went ahead with the questions. The figure before me was very dark and somewhat foreboding, with a pale face showing through a large dark robe and cowl with what looked like spiny black wings extending from its shoulders.

When I asked about its office, it remained still while saying and doing nothing. However, a glowing line seemed to streak diagonally across its body. I didn't understand what it was at first, but I continued to look closer. I repeated the question and the line seemed to brighten more. I followed it and was able to see it arc and widen at the top. Only then did I realize it was an illuminated scythe. Cassiel was holding it diagonally across his body with the blade to the upper left, and it somehow glowed against the shape of his black robes behind. There was also another glowing object in its right hand, which it kept towards its waist. I couldn't make out exactly what the object was because it just appeared to be a glowing light. I originally mistook it for a reflection of the candles' flame, but then realized it was unique to the vision. The angel's face was very white with deep shades of dark that marked its features. The glowing scythe pulsed from one end to the other and a trail of sectioned lights would move around the perimeter of the gold disk. This continued a few more times and it looked as if light was faintly pulsing around the perimeter in a counterclockwise motion. After a while, it occurred to me that the light and the sickle almost looked like the patterns of a clock that was moving backward.

I asked it to show me its true sign and character. Again, the image didn't move, but eventually faded to show a sickle in the top right, followed by an "h" looking symbol. I took this to be the Saturn symbol, but it looked slightly different than what I was used to. The image of the being faded to reveal a road with long wheat growing in fields in a rolling landscape. A human skull was underneath a path in the foreground and a figure was shooting an arrow, or throwing a spear, back toward the right. All these images sort of phased, one into the other, and I had trouble understanding everything I was seeing.

I asked the last question given in the list of interrogation questions to reveal if it was truly Cassiel. I never heard it speak; I only saw its image become more defined and fade out to show me another bizarre scene. I looked at this scene for quite some time, trying to comprehend what I was seeing. It was a horse running backward, heading toward the left, and three (or two and a half) riders were upon it. One was looking toward the left with its mouth open, looking shocked. The other was centered and looking straight at me, while the last seemed to morph into the second and was looking toward the right with a stern face. The heads were fairly distinct, but the bodies seemed to mesh together in a sort of grotesque appearance. The horse was very thin and sickly looking, but somehow seemed determined. This weird phasing scene went on for a while, then vanished to show the black, hooded angel with spiky dark wings, extending to the perimeter of the gold disk. It seemed very intent on me, but silent and unmoving. I felt wary, but I extended my mind toward it and spoke more from the heart, relating that I wished to integrate its beneficial offices into my being and practice. At this, I felt the atmosphere shift slightly and become less heavy. It was not oppressive by any means, but also not eager to expound upon my questions or inquiries. I asked for the assistance in a magical area that it was known to assist with. The angel raised the hand with the glowing orb or whatever it was and lifted it to the same height as the scythe. I took this as an affirmation, to my requests. The ritual was concluded shortly after I asked if I could record its seal and image in my Book of Spirits, of which it seemed to have no objection. I then recited the closing prayers and a personal one to God, in thanks of a successful operation.

The angel was not threatening in any way, but I was still very wary of its presence and capabilities. After the ritual, I drew Cassiel's image and wrote down everything I saw while it was still fresh in my mind. When I came upstairs, my wife asked if I had heard a scream. Evidently, she had heard someone scream and could not tell if it had come from outside or inside the house. I didn't recall hearing anything. She also said she noticed a rather odd odor in the house, perhaps from the incense.

The event had me puzzling over the images I saw for quite some time. The somewhat removed encounter of this planetary angel left me initially bewildered. I had to evoke him many times before feeling I knew what this angel was really about. However, my requests were indeed granted and materialized when I least expected them. Perhaps by design, this first evocation paved the way for more successful angelic encounters.

Cassiel

Conjuro & confirmo super vos Caphriel vel Cassiel, Machatori, & Seraquiel Angeli fortes & potentes: & per nomen Adonay, Adonay, Adonay, Eie, Eie, Eie, Acim, Acim, Acim, Cados, Cados, Ina vel Ima, Ima, Saday, Ja, Sar, Domini formatoris seculorum, qui in septimo die quievit: & per illum qui in beneplacito suo filiis Israel in hereditatem observandum dedit, ut eum firmiter custodirent, & sanctificarent, ad habendem inde bonam in alio seculo remunerationem: & per nomina Angelorum servientium in exercitu septimo Pooel Angelo magno & potenti principi: & per nomen stellæ quæ est Saturnus: & per sanctum Sigillum ejus: & per nomina praedicta conjuro super te Caphriel, qui præpositus es diei septimæ, quæ est dies Sabbati, quòd pro me labores, &c.

Agiel   Zazel

CHAPTER VIII

FURTHER REMARKS ABOUT SCRYING

fter corresponding with a number of dedicated and enthusiastic students of the DSIC system, I've come to appreciate the process that each individual struggles with attempting to work this system successfully. Despite their best efforts, rigorous adherence to tradition, process and application of the entire system, difficulties still arise for some. Unlocking the mind can be a lifelong pursuit in and of itself regardless of occult practices. If one is an enthusiastic magician but has little spiritual sight or sense for the "unseen" they may wish to focus solely on developing these capacities within themselves. Traditional and New Age books abound on various ways in which to do this. Many have been able to make breakthroughs in their magical work using the techniques these books offer while others find nothing seems to work for them.

To behold the intended spiritual audiences viably and clearly is the intended purpose of magical evocation so many are discouraged when they receive anything less. This point is understandable and has caused a great number of prospective magicians to abandon traditional practice or alter it entirely to an unrecognizable form. The phenomena of beholding a spirit is such that it has caused a considerable rift between occultists who have undergone the realization of witnessing spiritual phenomena and those who have yet to experience anything definable. The absence of any observable result from magical invocation/evocation can lead to compounded states of psychological doubt and disbelief despite the conscious efforts or desires to the contrary. For some, such lack of stimuli will cause them to leap directly into imagination, fantasy, or baseless alternatives just to not have to look failure in the face. Lack of apparent results is especially trying for westerners where entertainment and convenience is an ingrained expectation.

This multigenerational mindset of entitlement is extremely saturated in our culture coupled with little patience for developmental experience and work without observable benefits. Regardless of this dilemma, it is imperative that before you can ask something of a spirit you must first be certain of what or who it is you are asking. Therefore this magical operation cannot be successful without first having the proper capacities. The capacity for spiritual interaction and exchange is an ability that few are talented in and others have developed only after intense training. The human mind is an extremely complex mechanism and its faculties are beyond the scope of any one work. As relatable to mystical visions and perceptions however, some techniques do appear to assist many seeking to open their "inner eye".

There have been copious amounts of published material recently on the proper state of mind and process needed to be able to behold spiritual phenomena. In the event that you are planning to conduct these experiments without having previously experienced phenomena where a spirit was visually seen and audible heard, there will most likely be a measure of internal 'disbelief' and deep unconscious conditioning inhibiting the likelihood of you ever encountering such an event. A considerable amount of time will not only be needed to develop your astral senses but also in preparing your mind and spirit to be *allowed* to behold such occurrences. I use the word "allowed" because in my assessment, there indeed seems to be an unseen force or entity which moderates the level of exposure certain human beings are allotted concerning the supernatural. Often this force or entity is in an agreement with a deep part of the given person's psyche which for one reason or another is disallowed to the possibility of encountering spiritual phenomena. In many cases, people exhibit mindsets which are strictly adverse to any such contact. Those who are overly sarcastic, cynical, or skeptical in everyday circumstances will find it highly challenging to allow themselves to be open to the possibility of novel experiences. Many of us are duped into thinking this is a healthy and intelligent way to live and important to avoid appearing gullible or being victimized by a scam artists. Deeper introspection will show that these cynical attitudes are based on fear and disappointment. Such deep-seated emotions are unfavorable to genuine magical experience and will require no small amount of psychoanalysis and introspection.

The source of some inhibiting defense mechanisms in the deep unconscious has nothing to do with your conscious desires or affirmations that argue that you are ready to behold the supernatural. It's a rather odd paradox of systematic control in relation to your own physiological and sociological makeup as well as the outside moderations which help determine the appropriateness of your involvement in such matters. You cannot simply think away the earliest years of your life where your parents and society continually told you that there "are no monsters" or spooky things just to help you sleep at night. Mental conditioning is not something which fades away after early adulthood. In fact it only strengthens and becomes even more concreted with maturity. The ego of waking consciousness has little patience or acknowledgment for such concepts and wants to bypass even the mention of such hindrances as quickly as possible. Perhaps for good reason, no one is able to simply force their way past their own barriers by simply thinking on it. The only solution is to delve deep into the very occult centers of the simultaneous macrocosm and microcosm to unlock the doors of spiritual interaction. Naturally many shamanistic, spiritual and magical traditions are designed to do just this. As a note of encouragement, it's not so much the authenticity or workability of the tradition as it is much your ability to patiently and diligently work past your own barriers.

Often the best way toward a solution is to not focus on the problem but work toward developing a skill that will give you the necessary freedom to move beyond another barrier. For example, to overcome an overwhelming fear of heights it may not be productive to simply force yourself up on the roof of a skyscraper until you just "get over it". A more beneficial yet seemingly unrelated approach might be to just start with conscious, controlled breathing to lessen overall stress. This seemingly unrelated exercise when pursued frequently and with determination can lessen stress and anxieties in all fields and could even help in the overcoming of a phobia, simply through breathing. The exercise does not inherently have anything to do with "heights" but the source of the stress can be tackled from a similar standpoint. Likewise if you are frustrated at not being able to perceive even the slightest spiritual occurrence, beating your head against the wall over and over trying to "see something spiritual" may night be the best approach. However, by simply focusing on mental exercises which silence the mental chatter and distractions while completely absorbing oneself in stillness may be highly beneficial in developing the capacity in that part of the mind. This in turn allows one to experience spiritual phenomena without trying to unconsciously analyze, correct, distort, or dismiss the reality of the occurrence. This may be a difficult consideration for the eager magician who wants to jump right in and experience the full splendor of the celestial angels right away, but magic has and will continue to work within the framework of reality.

A magical student of mine recently had trouble accepting the variation between my experiences and that of my scryer's to his own. He comment- ed that he would only receive apparent atmospheric changes and intuitive perceptions and then would eventually see elaborate geometric shapes and patters after the angels were invoked. He didn't consider this to be successful however and remained frustrated through many of his early evocations. Such signs should be appreciated as evidence of progress and that they energies are acknowledging your summons and intentions. However it is admittedly difficult for a human being to communicate to geometric shapes and emo- tional perceptions alone so this should not be a stopping point either. Early experiences should also *not* be considered incorrect or a failure in any way as the sensations as well as any shapes and imagery most likely hold vital clues and information to your method of communication and understanding. The real task then becomes not in seeing what you expect but begin completely devoid of judgment and expectation and taking the experience as it unfolds. If the ritual exhibits absolutely no palpable manifestations, sensations or al- terations in atmosphere, consciousness or observable reality, you still have something to work with. I do not suggest abandoning the experiment and closing it without proper follow through and petition. I actually encourage beginners to speak aloud to the intended entities and asking for assistance to see and communicate with them better. Follow through with the entire ritual as if everything is going to plan but abandon all concerns with result or feedback for the time being. In this was you will be able to follow through with a ritual uninterrupted by your own mind and concerns about results so that when the spirit does begin to manifest itself to you, you will not be shocked or interrupted by your own awe.

As I have alluded to earlier in my chapter on scrying, my personal ob- serving and communicating with spiritual entities appeared to go through various psychological stages of mental and emotional alterations. Initially communication was fragmented and certain aspects weather sight or hear- ing would fluctuate during the course of the operation. I found that the longer I was able to keep my mind in a neutral state and just receive the in- formation that was coming across, the better the overall interaction went. To fully understand how this works its best to understand how human beings interact with one another. For most of us we are designed to communicate at several different levels at once, picking up on auditory, visual and subtle cues that give us far more information than what is simply being said by another person. In conjunction with this we are also filtering through several different layers of judgments, critiques and discerning analytical behavior which causes us to more or less perceive the entire experience based on a multitude of internal functioning which have more to do with our emotional and intellectual predisposition than the reality of the actual event. When these filters become active during a spiritual encounter, its unsurprising that the event is even more filtered with our imagination filling in the blanks of that which we can simply not comprehend at the time. As I mentioned before, some people seem to have a more natural capacity to decode the information and fill in the blanks spots than do others.

We need to accept that spirits or angels do not look like anything perceivable or comprehendible in their natural state and that the anthropomorphic images we see have more to do with our acceptable forms of communication. For the historical occultist, it was more about the knowledge and results (benefits) the spirit could relate rather than the clarity of the appearance and definability of the spirit. For those like me however, the experience and interaction is of monumental importance and is an element not able to be overlooked. If simply relying on the accounts of the scryer and receiving the second hand knowledge is not good enough, dedication to developing your astral or spiritual sight should take the majority of your magical practice before conducting more complex invocations or evocations. Perceiving colors and geometric shapes are probably closer to the angel's true 'visual natures' but people communicate best when they interact with beings which are more socially familiar i.e., other human beings. Another suggestion develop this ability is to train your mental imagery through magical and imagination practices which can be found in a variety of traditions and magical source works.

If you find yourself at and end all place of frustration and disappointment than you may be at the point where a psycho-spiritual breakthrough is required to move past the veil of the mundane. I know of no better way to do this than to undertake the operation to unite with your Holy guardian Angel or (HGA). The book of Abrameline the Mage is the primary source for this experiment and if you are interested, I suggest you purchase a copy of "The Holy Guardian Angel" by *Nephilim Press* in which I share my own account of going through this rather intense magical undertaking.

Recording An Invocation

An idea I initially found offensive has since come under the category necessity in practice for my work. Since my evocations have exploded into multiple hour long session of extensive question and answer as well as complex replies of valuable information I have cased trying to rely solely on my handwriting speed to capture all the information which comes across. During a few of the early operations I began missing points and not recording each word or image which came across. It was difficult to keep up with the often rapid and overwhelming bombardment of information which the angels graciously conveyed to me and my scryer simultaneously and I did not want to miss a single concept which seems valuable beyond measure. I wasn't willing to settle for short hand notes this since each word, experience, and image seemed to capture an enormity of wisdom for me. Especially during my first rounds of DSIC experiments where I was scrying and operating at the same time my interaction and retention of the encounters were often blurred. The information seemed to fade swiftly after the operation was finished like waking from a dream. Obviously a better way had to be adopted to accurately record the lengthy events of the conjurations and I was willing to consider modern technological devices.

I began arranging an audio recorder within the circle to record the voices of myself, or scryer and anything else which may show up on the recording as solid record of what transpire during and after the operation. I keep the recorder going directly after the ritual so my scryer and I can reflect on the most pertinent visions and interactions which took place while they are still fresh in our heads. This way we can relate everything we are able to by speaking it aloud. For quite some time I was against having any modern technological devices included in magical workings of any kind due to their unreliability and inability to capture the entirety of events visible and invisible which occurs during an operation. I'm also still firmly of the belief that invocation/evocation and magica in general is not a spectator sport but a deeply personal involvement which cannot be ratified by an outside observer. Regardless, I've been finding more and more occurrences which seem to be captured on an audio recording. My practice has been to review the audio recording on the following day or closest day following when I have time and transcribe everything into written format. In this way I can go back and review sections of the operation at any time and if I wish, insert related results and circumstances which pertained to the operation.

I should state that I am not strictly against video recording a magical experiment either but will caution the reader not to jump to that as a necessary instrument for evocation. In these days of the paranormal media craze and adrenaline seeking examples of paranormal evidence, the magician is not a paranormal investigator but an active participant in the entirety of the phenomena which takes place in apparent, subtle, intrinsic as well as external ways. Do not rely on recording devices on any kind to verify a magical ceremony for you. Use them to verify the details and information which transpired and possibly pick up aspects you may have overlooked. Remember a magician is not one who goes seeking evidence of the paranormal, they are an active participant in the "paranormal" and move from the point of verification which begins and ends in the centermost point of their own consciousness.

THE RITUAL DEBRIEF AND RECORD

After every magical operation a "ritual debrief" is highly recommended. Whether you conducted your evocation solo or with a scryer it is important to digest exactly what all occurred during your experience. Many times so much activity will occur that certain points will be overlooked. It's important to go over every detail as best as you remember it, regardless if the entire operation was audio recorded or not. As described previously, the angels and spirit's methods of communication is multifold. Make sure to recall and record all feelings, images, sensations and inspirations which may have occurred during the exchange. Often a vital piece of information is overlooked during the ecstasy of the ritual itself, only to be recalled afterword, and its importance clarified. Through the ritual debrief you will be able to organize and highlight the important points of the ritual and the results to follow. Being a good magician is being a good record keeper and data recorder. From habits picked up keeping a dream journal and going back and connecting the dots, the diligent magician should have copious and organized notes from each experiment. Another common trend I have found among western magicians is the entertainment mentality. That is they look forward to the stimuli, the appearance, the presence, the paranormal or supernatural phenomena, and then once it's over and done with its soon forgotten or at least the reason of the operation is long sense passed. Keeping magical record may indeed be the indicator for further magical success of abandonment. There is a fine point in the progressive behavior of the magician which will indicate serious interest and dedication or a desire to simply experience an adrenaline rush of the unusual.

The diligent occultist will continue with operation after operation, often evoking or invoking different entities continuously as a matter of introduction and curiosity. A continual hunger to become more familiar with that which is unknown is without doubt a major motivating factor for the spirit conjurer. In the midst of this undertaking, previous operations can often be overlooked and/or forgotten if not reviewed methodically after some time has lapsed. In just about every instance when I have gone back and reread or listened to a previous operation I end up being struck with some revelation which I somehow glossed over the first few times around. During many of these occurrences, something will stick out which happens to have relevance to what is going on in my life at the present. Assuming a spirit will only divulge information which strikes your interest and purpose at the time of the operation is a bit naive at best. For one spirits do not function within the same framework and conception of time as humans do. The liner concept of time is even debatable among corporeal intelligences in fact. Review and meditate on previous operations on a regular basis regardless if you are convinced that you digesting the full meaning and purpose of that working.

THE ALTAR CANDLE LIGHTER AND SNUFFER

A ritual tool which is highly appropriate and in line with the other Catholic ritual paraphernalia of the ceremony is an alter candle lighter and snuffer. The device which is typically around three feet in length and has a large candle snuffer on one side and an extendable wick for lighting on the other is ideal for this particular ceremony if not all magical ritual in general. For one, it allows you to light the two altar candles on either side of the holy table and pedestal with ease without having to awkwardly lean or step over the circle. If you are working with a partner/scryer, it allows you to light the candles without crowding and disturbing them during the ceremony. Another benefit is that it is a little bit more formal and appropriate to the work than the "click-click" of a grill lighter or the sulfurous spark of matches. As long as there is wick left, the end of the lighter portion usually stays lit and extends to the wick of your tappers or charcoal with ease. After using it in a few rituals I would say the altar lighter is. The church lighters are not exactly inexpensive to purchase but are highly advantageous and worth it in my experience. The only point to be aware of is to be sure the wick from the altar lighter is extinguished after use and that it is placed neatly and respectfully within the circle but away from where it could be knocked over or tripped over during the ceremony. I find the best place to put it is directly next to me on the small table I keep within the circle where I copy down notes and have my book of Spirits.

Your ritual candle lighter and snuffer should be stored away when not in use and never used to light candles (or put them out) for reasons other than use in direct ceremony. Extra wicks should be kept with your ritual vestments and tools and if you wish consecrated to these ends as well. It will also be necessary to clean the candle snuffer after each use in ceremony to avoid getting soot or wax over your other magical paraphernalia and vestments. Attentiveness and respectful mindfulness for each piece of magical equipment and procedure will go a long way in your practice.

THE HOLY LAMP

As an additional piece of equipment, the Holy lamp of ceremonial magick is in item I have not omitted through my many years of practice. It services as more than just the "spiritual light" in the center of the circle. It also acts as the necessary light to read from the book of conjurations, to see questions which were written down, and to write down notes or responses from the angels/spirits. Besides this, I am in the habit of lighting the charcoals for the incense as well as the two tapper candles on the altar from my central Holy lamp. When not in use, the lamp remains on my altar in my magical chamber and its function and meaning remain constant regardless of being used in magical ritual or simply as a votive. Years ago I experimented with some ideas of combining holy oils with the oil lamp fuel as an added consecration to the light begin emitted and have since very much enjoyed the effects and continue to re-consecrate and blend holy oil with the fuel every time the lamp needs refilling. My personal blend for my holy lamp is as follows: 3 drops Holy Abrameline oil, 1 drop olive anointing oil, one drop hyssop anointing oil, 3 drops frankincense oil. I don't suggest adding more than the suggested drops as the oils do not readily mix that well with the lamp oil and may affect how well it burns. However in the suggested dosage, the oils mix easily with a half cup of lamp oil and give it almost a glowing yellow color which seems perfect for the holy light. IT will be such that you will be able to notice the faint aroma of the oils as well and they will burn and emit their sense through the lamp through the chamber which is very agreeable.

The holy lamp or light should be treated as the title suggests and never lit or used for mundane purposes. When not used specifically for magical ritual I would suggest only lighting it on holy days or times when giving direct attention to the overall sanctity of your altar is suitable. Issue your most heightened prayers and intentions of devotion toward its light when you are in the midst of holy invocation or prayer. Let the entirety of the matter, function and intention of your holy lamp be that of pure divinity and sacredness. A room or chamber lit by the flame of it will reach into every dark corner of the mundane and imbue it with the holy light of the spirit as well. Likewise, when the candle tappers and charcoals are lit from this divine light, the transfer of divine energy will not be lost on the operation or the spirits involved. I have found it an indispensible inclusion to my DSIC practice and have enjoyed the immense benefits from its use.

AN EVOLVING PRACTICE

Directly before the operation both my scryer and I will wash our hands and face in a ritualistic manner, I recite the 51st Psalm verse 7 out of frequent use as a purification of cleansing and centering. We both don our albs and ritual vestments respectively and I complete the final temple arrangements within the circle. My scryer will sit on the small wooden stool which is cushioned for comfort due to long scrying sessions. When I put on my stole and lamen I also give a parchment copy of the spirit's sigil to my scryer to hold and meditate on. Before the actual invocations I take a long moment in stillness. My scryer will begin to focus solely on entering the deepest state of trance and astral sight as possible. About this time I anoint my forehead in the sign of the cross with holy oil reciting the *trinitarian formula* in Latin: "In nomine Patris, et Filii, et Spiritūs Sancti", and do the same to my scryer. I follow by placing my hands lightly on his head and issue a silent blessing that he will be able to see and interact with the angels successfully and clearly and that his sight and hearing will be tuned to their wisdom and council. I return back to a moment of silence which feel can be overlooked by those new to evocation as the excitement and anticipation builds, making sure all the proper elements are in order and hoping all will go as planned. The magus or operator might begin to develop unneeded chatter, unconscious feelings of anxiety or doubt, or simple distractions which are not beneficial for the ritual. In this moment of silence I take as long as is needed without consideration on the matter. A feeling of undeniable intention and power swells from my center when it is time to begin and I move from that point till it issues forth as spoken words through the invocation.

I've had a few readers inquire if I used the traditional words of the invocation and questions each and every time. The answer to this is that I usually will do but after memorizing them I speak them from a point of fluid familiarity and will often change wording or add extra phrasing and wordage to fit the uniqueness of the ceremony and spirit being called upon. Also, I often change the words "command" or demand" when dealing with angels since this has not seemed appropriate in my dealing with them. I will typically say "appear to us visibly here in this crystal, and answer our *inquires*" (instead of commands). I still stick to much of the original wording and phrasing as I think it inherently contains power and consensus for the ritual and gives a level of important consistency through each invocation. A magical invocation is a litany of divine structure and movement. When it is truly spoken through the magical voice and intent of the magician it literally moves the occult constructs of the universe. They are the most divine song, the true meaning of the Spell. The invocation when memorized and integrated becomes a cherished and potent tool of extreme power and authority. In correct use, it only becomes stronger with each recitation as understanding and integration increase.

The previously unwritten symphony of the magical operation consists of a multitude of divinely harmonizing elements which when properly tuned, reverberate with the sound of intention issuing from the voice of the magus/operator. The sound should hum and reinforce the intention through the magician's wand held in the hand, through the lamen and necklace around his neck, through the circle and all apparatus therein to the very altar and crystal within the pedestal itself. The magician's song through divine invocation should reach and touch each participating element in perfect pitch. For the striving magician, unwilling to settle for ambiguous experiences and sensations during magical operations, the mind and senses must be opened in ways to make each operation and experience undeniable.

During one of his DSIC operations my student received keen insight as to the use and purpose of the grimoric tools he stated that, "the tools serve as an aid to deepen and direct one's astral senses. In this sense, the crystal serves as a focal point for the operator's intrinsic spiritual sight. In other words, it is a mirror that reflects one's spiritual sight, so the intensity of the vision will depend on the operator's level of development." I believe this was stated beautifully and very accurately as well. Such inspiration and insight into the hidden (occult) meaning of your practice and implements in magical ritual will come with serious practice and consideration over time. The more you thoroughly involve yourself and become intimately familiar with the practices and process of the ritual, the more it will become your own and the subtle and hidden aspects revealed to you. This benefit is not something that can be simply taught or read about, only experienced with practice and earnest involvement.

Dedicate yourself fully to the work and consider that each component of the ritual, from the vestments, to the multitude of magical paraphernalia, and lengthy invocations, is honoring the reality of the events and beings they are intended for. Do not let any part become simply an adherence to tradition or formality. Instead let the formality be an iatrical part of your practice to show true respect and appreciation for not only the beings invoked, but for the true divinity within yourself. Treat magical practice as the most sacred art and it will blossom as a sacred resounding blessing in your life. Don't waste time worrying about the results of living up to your expectations and time spent investing in the system. A sharp suit and attentive demeanor does not automatically make you a good business man but it's an excellent start as well as outward representation of the correct attitude. Many feel called to ritual magical for a select number of reasons. Many will become discouraged and abandon the practice if they do not immediately show signs which match their expectations. However, for the select few who preserver without succumbing to disappointment, a hidden world will begin to reveal itself in ways never before imagined.

FURTHER REMARKS ABOUT SCRYING

In the upcoming companion to Gateways Through Stone and Circle and the continuation of the amazing system known as "Drawing Spirits into Crystals" the author will be revealing a complete wealth of personal accounts. The second volume will contain word for word relations of the experiences he and his scryer underwent during remarkable invocations as well as other relatable events. It will span over three years of continual magical operations and some of the most amazing encounters either one has ever encountered. Not only will the reader be able to read detailed first had accounts of the appearances and dialog from all seven planetary archangels, they will also learn how to fashion talismans, and conduct magical methods that have never been revealed previously. Learn about the origins of the archangels as they describe it themselves! Follow along the actual written records of Frater Ashen Chassan and his amazing scryer, Ben Willman as they follow up on the instructions given by the archangels which reveal truths and magical power far beyond either of them could ever anticipate. The relation in this book may read like a fantastical novel at times by each is an accurate relation of what both underwent during these remarkable experiences with the Archangels and other spirits.

CONCLUSION

ith each completed ritual comes a deeper understanding of how DSIC is supposed to flow from beginning to end. Scrying improves with each direct effort like a honed skill. Comprehension of the symbols and words the angels relate become more discernible over time. From the crafting of the implements to their proper use in the intended ritual, the entire art form becomes vibrant and vital to your spirit. Although I have worked with planetary intelligences before, nothing has compared to the intensity of this system. The angelic beings seem to appreciate the sincerity and effort involved in contacting them in this manner. More than making demands, the angels increase their level of communication if they are shown a sincere effort to hold frequent audience. Traditional ritual magic seems to evolve into an intense practice of devotion, with direct experience of the divine rather than receiving it secondhand.

There is no limit to what can be learned from working with these angels and spirits. Continual incorporation of their beneficial attributes will develop your being and lifestyle like you wouldn't believe. If sought with correct intention, untainted by the delusions of fantasy or self-fulfilling glorification (remember that Trithemius' prayer in the Invocation prohibits such acts of selfishness), I have no doubt you will achieve the extent of your highest aspirations.

When matched with the proper movement of the stars and their seasons, frequent invocation will yield increasingly wondrous results. Drawing upon each angel's attributes in the proper time will put you in sync with the movements of creation. Just like the creation of each magical item, the Invocation/Evocation operation is a process that grows in amplitude and refinement over time. With earnest work to develop a finely finished product, you will notice the benefits increase dramatically. This is not a "one shot art," I'm afraid. This practice was only meant for those who had the time and dedication to accomplish such tedious efforts.

I'm continually discovering the ways in which these angelic beings can assist in every endeavor I undertake. I recommend evoking each of the angels multiple times during its season of aligned rule, i.e., during the corresponding planet's most profitable, day, hour, season, and cycle. During these times, evoke the angel with the intention of open learning, rather than what you can "get from them." Don't assume you know what the angel can or will do for you. Initially, you may be surprised at how well these beings know you and what they will offer, without having to ask for it. Be open and attentive to the advice they relate and how to best utilize their offices within your life. Keep the information, which is meant only for you, to yourself. Honor the exchange that has taken place and share it only with the most trusted of people.

When true evocation of an angelic is achieved, just being in the presence of these mighty beings will begin to alter your consciousness and perspective on life. There is so much more than the mundane goings-on of the base world. So much is to be learned and accomplished. I hope this art leads you to the fullest manifestations of those dreams, even if they are not known to you yet.

Grimoric magic is a process of trial and error, relationship and learning. It differs from a sterile scientific experiment in which one might get the desired reaction and then move on to something else. The extent to any art is the effort of experience put in over time. The experience in these operations is what makes it worthwhile. Knowing that you have contacted something that, at first, you weren't entirely convinced even existed is what makes you continue. Don't expect to have all the answers after one encounter, because in truth, you will not have them even after a hundred encounters.

Keep your mind and heart open to what is received, for most times, it will not match your expectations.

Contemplate the things you learn from these beings, but be careful not to obsess over any of them. An Operator/Magician should be well-researched, organized, and prepared before attempting any serious magical practice, especially those of Invocation/Evocation. Times of previous frustration with this art stemmed from a few variables I have come to recognize and will share with you here.

CONCLUSION

1. The operation may not proceed well if you enter it with expectations of a reward or proof. Having these desires as a main motivator has never helped in any of my practices.

2. Trying to force Archangels into anything is a sure way to receive nothing at all and possibly something counter to what you desired later on. I haven't tried the above, but am quite convinced of this point, regardless. Even in working with lesser spirits or intelligences, have a clear understanding of what is in their capability.

3. Lacking in sincerity and belief equals lacking in *will* where magical practice is concerned. You need your will to be completely focused on the operation without any doubts or distractions. By the time you are ready to perform the art of DSIC, you should be familiar with the entire process and procedure. Remember, you're the active participant in this operation and cannot perform it from an objective standpoint. Within your magic circle, you stand at the axis to divine connection. It is you who will initiate this connection.

However you decide to utilize this art and operation, and whatever aspects you decide to integrate into your practice, will be, of course, up to you. I have vied to follow the written operation as closely to the text as possible and have had no regrets. No other modified forms of magic have come close to what this system offers. There is no substitute for conducting the experiment yourself and undergoing the experiences that await you.

No author's dictates should be taken to heart without question. I have simply offered the discoveries of my own undertakings as I experienced them. I have described those principles that seemed vital to grimoric ceremonial magic as I understand them. Each act of magic is inherently personal for it to have any importance in the life of the magician. In the practice of grimoric magic and reproducing ceremonial practices described in the text, we must accept what the author's original intentions were without trying to displace them with watered down, modern conceptions.

BIBLIOGRAPHY

Agrippa, Heinrich Cornelius and Stephen Skinner. *Fourth Book of Occult Philosophy*. Askin Publishers, 2005.

Barrett, Francis. *The Magus, Book II*. London, 1801.

Brand, N. L. *The Abbot Trithemius*. Leiden: Brill, 1981.

Brann, Noel. *Trithemius and Magical Theology: A Chapter in the Controversy over Occult Studies in Early Modern Europe*. Albany: State University of New York Press, 1999.

Christel, Steffen. "Untersuchungen zum "Liber de scriptoribus ecclesiasticis" des Johannes Trithemius", Aus: Archiv für Geschichte des Buchwesens Bd 10, Lfg 4 - 5 [1969] 1247 - 1354.

Hockley, Frederick. *A Complete Book of Magic Science*. The Teitan Press, 2008.

Hockley, Frederick. *Occult Spells A Nineteenth Century Grimoire*. The Teitan Press, 2009.

Kahn, David. *The Codebreakers: the Story of Secret Writing*. 1967, 2nd edition 1996. pp. 130–137. ISBN 0-684-83130-9.

Kuhn, Rudolf. *Großer Führer durch Würzburgs Dom und Neumünster: mit Neumünster-Kreuzgang und Walthergrab*. 1968. p. 108.

Leitch, Aaron. "Ananael Blog." Web. http://aaronleitch.wordpress.com/tag/aaron-leitch.

Peterson, Joseph. "Johannes Trithemius: The art of drawing spirits into crystals." *Twilit Grotto: Archives of Western Esoterica,* 2011. Web. http://www.esotericarchives.com/tritheim/trchryst.htm.

Skinner, Stephen and David Rankine. *Veritable Key of Solomon.* Llewellyn Publications, 2008.

Warnock, Christopher. "Johannes Trithemius Main Page." *Renaissance Astrology,* 2000. Web. http://www.renaissanceastrology.com/trithemius.html.

Wolfe, James Raymond. *Secret Writing: the Craft of the Cryptographer.* New York: McGraw-Hill, 1970. pp. 112–114.

---. "Archangel Correspondences." ArchAn Publishing, 2011. Web. http://www.archangels-and-angels.com/aa_pages/correspondences/archangels_corresp_index.html.

---. "eBay." Web. www.ebay.com.

---. "Gentlemen for Jupiter." Web. http://www.gentlemenforjupiter.com/.

---. "Johannes Trithemius." Wikipedia, the free encyclopedia. Accessed 2011.

---. "Pergamena." Web. http://www.pergamena.net/products/parchment/.

---. "Planetary Hours Calculator." Astrology. Web. http://www.astrology.com.tr/planetary-hours.asp.

CPSIA information can be obtained at www.ICGtesting.com
Printed in the USA
BVOW03s0003310316

442294BV00004B/142/P